FRIENDS
OF ACPL

P9-EMJ-652

3 1833 02619 5278

J
CARRIS, JOAN DAVENPORT.
BEWARE THE RAVENS, AUNT
MORBELIA

BEWARE THE RAVENS,
Aunt Morbelia

BEWARE THE RAVENS,
Aunt Morbelia

JOAN CARRIS

LITTLE, BROWN AND COMPANY
BOSTON   NEW YORK   TORONTO   LONDON

First Edition

Library of Congress Cataloging-in-Publication Data

Carris, Joan Davenport.
    Beware the ravens, Aunt Morbelia / Joan Carris.
       p.   cm.
    Summary: Todd Fearing, his aunt Morbelia, and his friend Jeff are
shadowed by mysterious characters when they visit London and their
ancestral home.
    ISBN 0-316-12961-5
    [1. Aunts — Fiction.   2. London (England) — Fiction.   3. Mystery and
detective stories.]   I. Title.
PZ7.C2347Be   1995
[Fic] — dc20   94-25654

                    10   9   8   7   6   5   4   3   2   1

                              RRD-VA

                 Printed in the United States of America

ACKNOWLEDGMENTS
AND AUTHOR'S NOTE

A great big THANK YOU to my English readers and friends, Jan Bradley, Head Teacher at Pirbright County Middle School, and Pat Baylis, who may never be allowed to completely retire from teaching.

I have tried to be true to historic fact, leaving monuments, streets, and museums intact as far as I know, but this is a work of fiction. I created pubs and towns and tea shops as necessary. The characters are likewise fictional.

JOAN CARRIS

1

The Ancestral Pile

Todd and Jeff squeezed through the narrow doorway into the tiny airplane lavatory. "Boy, they sure don't waste any space on bathrooms," Todd observed. He put the toilet lid down and sat on it, legs folded.

Jeff squinted into the mirror over the sink. "We've been on this jet forever." He began splashing cold water on his face.

"We don't land till ten, London time," said Todd, looking at his watch. He yawned so widely he wasn't sure he could pull out of it.

"Ah-ah-ah!" Jeff shook a warning finger in his face. "You let in fifty devils for sure. You simply *must* remember to cover your mouth." He managed to sound just like Todd's Aunt Morbelia, who was snoring efficiently in her seat in the main cabin. As soon as the dinner trays had been cleared a few hours ago, she had pulled up her blanket, put on the British Airways eyemask, and willed herself to sleep. That's how she was.

Todd still wasn't sure Jeff knew what he had let himself in for. A trip to England sounded great, of course. A trip to England with his Great-Aunt Morbelia, well, that would be something else again.

Through another yawn he said, "Jeff, she's a teacher, remember? She could lecture the whole trip!"

"Not to worry, Todd-baby. Aunt Morbelia and I get along great." Jeff gave him a friendly punch in the chest. "But you better move now, because I've really got to — "

"I'm moving! I'm moving!"

Todd took his turn at the sink. Being in this tiny space with Jeff was like being in a school locker with an elephant, he decided. Out in the main cabin, though, even the quietest joking around had gotten them dirty looks from people trying to sleep. At least in here they could talk.

Over the flushing noise of the toilet Jeff said, "Where do you think this stuff goes?" A violently blue liquid swirled round and round in the stainless steel bowl. "They don't just open a hole on the bottom of the plane and let it — "

"I sure hope not. But they used to on trains, Grampa says. He drank quarts and quarts of water before they went on a trip, he said, just so he could watch the train tracks go by while he peed on them. And a sign in the men's room said, DO NOT FLUSH WHEN TRAIN IS IN STATION."

Jeff made a face. "How'd you like to live real near some of those old train tracks?"

The Fasten Seatbelts sign came on, sending them back to their seats. Aunt Morbelia, awake and alert, was tucking in a few white strands of hair that had dared to stray from her bun during the night. "Good morning, boys. Breakfast is on its way. How did you sleep?"

"We didn't." Todd shrugged.

"Oh, my. Well, a driver is meeting us at Heathrow with a hire car, and we shall be at Harrowwood — that is the Fearing estate — in an hour. You may rest then if you want."

"The Fearing estate," echoed Jeff. "Wow."

Aunt Morbelia gave a small, refined snort. "I should not be impressed if I were you, Jeff. Harrowwood is a mouldering old pile of stone that has been nothing but a problem since I inherited it. I am amazed the estate agent suggested we stay there. Of course, I have to see it again before deciding what to do with it." She sighed. "Managing property at long distance is never very satisfactory."

Half in jest, Todd said, "Does it have forests and a game warden and poachers like in the movies?"

"I cannot promise any poachers, and the game-keeper is gone now, but there are acres of beautiful woods. We even had some crazy relatives . . . once upon a time." She smiled in memory. "You would have liked Cousin Albert, Todd. He was a wonderful person. After I had moved to America, though, he was incarcerated, the poor dear."

"Burned up?" Todd asked.

"Burned up is *incinerated*," Jeff said carefully. Jeff helped Todd, who was dyslexic, with words, and in turn Todd helped Jeff with math and science.

"He was incarcerated in the insane asylum. That is when the estate passed to me and my sisters," Aunt Morbelia went on. "He was harmless, of course, but he felt passionately about animals' rights. That is more common now, but back then it probably made some unimaginative people think he was abnormal."

"Probably," said Todd, only half listening. He was visualizing the "mouldering old pile of stone" and the vast woods. When the croissants, muffins, and soury orange juice came, he ate hungrily. At last he was having a real vacation. Until now, he had spent every summer in the Hampshire Learning Center with other dyslexic kids.

"Dad and I'll miss you something awful, but have a super time, honey. You earned it," his mom had said, hugging him in front of half the world at the Cincinnati airport.

Jeff's mom, who was one of those firm kind of mothers, had said, "You'll change planes in Washington, Jeff, so for heaven's sake keep track of your ticket. Remember that people going into seventh grade are *half grown*. We expect you to use your heads at home, but especially when you go to a foreign country."

"It is *not a foreign country*. It is *England*," Aunt Morbelia protested.

"Yes, dear, we know." Todd's dad hugged her. "I'm sure the boys will behave, but if you need me for any reason at all, I'll be on the next plane out of here. Just . . . um . . . don't be surprised at the changes, okay? It's been a few decades since you lived there."

The jet landed at ten in the morning at Heathrow airport, outside of London. Todd, Jeff, and Aunt Morbelia entered the terminal and stood in the lines marked for visitors to the United Kingdom. After inching forward for some time, Jeff said, "I guess everybody in the world comes here, hunh?"

"I guess," Todd replied, fascinated by the baggy pants, the amazing varieties of turbans and hairdos, the strange shoes, and the tiny girls in saris that flitted around the entrance hall like pastel butterflies.

Eventually they arrived at desk number six. The official studied Aunt Morbelia's and Todd's passports. Both photos showed people with prominent cheekbones in long, narrow faces. Both had dark, deep-set eyes, large noses, and wide mouths. "Hi ho, here's a family resemblance," the man said.

Jeff snickered and Todd elbowed him in the ribs.

Aunt Morbelia gave the man a look that would have withered anyone but a passport offical.

At last the man said, "Very good, madam," and stamped each passport. "Enjoy your stay in the U.K."

After retrieving their luggage, Todd pushed their loaded cart past customs inspection and out through swinging doors to the meeting area. In the crowd that jockeyed for a better view of the newcomers stood a tall, white-haired stick of a man in a faded black suit. He was holding up a sign that said FEARING.

"Morbelia Fearing! Over here!" With an imperious, gloved hand, she summoned the man in black.

"Down the end, mum," he replied, motioning to his right where the railings ended. There he removed his cap and bobbed his head at Aunt Morbelia, but he did not smile. "Follow me, mum." To Todd he said, "I'll take that cart."

The three travelers did their best to keep up with his long strides on the way to the garage. Very soon they were installed in the wide backseat of a stately, dark green car, and their luggage was stowed in the boot. Silently, the driver took them out of the garage and southwest into Surrey.

Todd saw the man's eyes in the rearview mirror as he snatched quick glimpses of his passengers, but he offered no information or even a welcome. Aunt Morbelia was busy frowning, first out the right window, then out the left. Jeff put his head back against the plush gray upholstery and went to sleep. His mouth sagged open, and he snored softly.

Too keyed up to sleep, Todd fidgeted between them. "I guess you can't take pictures out of a car window," he said, gripping the camera his parents had given him as a going-away present.

"Nothing here is worth photographing," said his aunt. "I cannot *believe* what I am seeing. Once this was forest and rolling fields. Now it is concrete . . . and filthy buildings . . . and high-speed motorways. It is *inexcusable*."

Todd said, "Let's forget this part, okay? The rest of England's probably great, like it always was, like the estate. Aunt Morbelia, how come your family didn't live there instead of up in Yorkshire?"

"My father was the younger brother, that is why. The older brother, Albert Leatherhead Fearing — "

"*Leatherhead?*"

"Yes — his mother's maiden name — Celtic in origin. Now, as I was saying, back then the older brother always inherited the property, so Albert and his family lived on the estate. He was the father of poor, deranged Cousin Albert, the chap I mentioned before."

"But you said the estate's big. Why didn't they share it?"

Aunt Morbelia's expression darkened. "My uncle, Albert Leatherhead, was an evil man. That is why we lived far away. The brothers looked alike, as all the Fearings do, and Father was afraid of being accused of Albert's crimes by mistake."

"Geez, what'd he do?"

"He eliminated people," she said with a discreet chopping motion. "At least that is what Father told us. He was sure the woods on the estate were full of shallow graves.

"We made some visits here while I was growing up, but we never came back after my grandmother's seventieth birthday. A year later, my parents died in the influenza epidemic, and I moved to America with my sisters, as you know."

Unreal, Todd thought, thinking of her casual reference to graves on the estate. She was completely at home — even happy at times — with anything ghoulish or supernatural.

Given his choice, Todd preferred laughter to shivers, but after several months of living with her, he was used to his aunt's morbid interests. "Is Harrowwood haunted, then?" he asked.

She thought briefly. "I doubt it. Certainly not the south wing where we shall be. I need to inspect the property, as you know, and I have family papers to see to — that sort of thing. We shall move to London at the weekend."

As the car purred southwest on the dual carriageway, Todd leaned back and gave in to sleep. When he woke up, the car door was ajar and he heard voices from outside. He poked Jeff until he, too, was awake, and both of them stared out the window at what could only be the Fearing estate.

"Oh, man, is this for real?" whispered Jeff.

Crumbling gray stone towers marked either end of the huge old manor house, which was three tall stories. A square center portion rose yet another story, with slim, dark towers on both sides of it. Tiny, leaded panes formed the windows, which looked as if they hadn't been washed in a century. It was all a depressing gray stone, except for the parts covered with green mold or black mildew.

Just then, cawing in harsh alarm, three large black birds flew out of a broken window, high up in the far left tower.

"Ah, what an unfortunate omen!" cried Aunt Morbelia. "Ravens in the north tower."

2

Cousin Albert's Legacy

Whoa, thought Todd, staring at the ominous pile of stone. What a perfect setting for a horror movie.

He was imagining a ghost drifting out of a third-story window when suddenly he felt as if someone were watching him. When he looked around, he saw the driver peering in at him — examining him almost — through the rear window of the car.

Instinctively Todd frowned. The driver jerked upright, raised the trunk lid, and disappeared from view.

You'd think he'd never seen an American before, Todd thought, as he and Jeff joined Aunt Morbelia on the front steps. She was banging the brass door knocker on the massive oak door, and while they waited, he considered the knocker. The horned head with bulging eyes and cruel mouth stared ferociously back at him from its post on the door. "Aunt Morbelia, what is that thing?"

"A gargoyle, like the ones up on the rain gutters. Step out into the courtyard and look up at the others. I always thought they were a nice touch, myself. Oh, where *is* that man?" She banged the brass gargoyle until, had it been a real creature, it would have begged for mercy.

And at last the door creaked open. A small man in a navy pinstriped suit leaned toward them, blinking his pale blue eyes as he said, "Is that you, Miss Fearing?"

"Of course it is I! And you are Peter Swallow?"

"Well . . . I was yesterday." He chuckled. "Do forgive me. I've always fancied a good joke." He put a hand to his chest as if the hilarity of it all was too much for him.

Aunt Morbelia's eyes flashed. "We should like to come inside. The boys and I are tired and — "

"You brought toys?" Mr. Swallow cupped his right ear in his hand and leaned forward.

"I said *boys!*" Her voice rose dangerously. "*These boys* — standing here in front of you! We all need to *rest!* You wrote that we should stay here, remember?"

If this guy's the one in charge, no wonder the place is a wreck, Todd thought. "Hi," he said to Mr. Swallow. "This is Jeff Lorimer and I'm Todd Fearing." He held out his hand.

Mr. Swallow came toward the voice, bumped into the hand, and grasped it warmly. "How do ye do, then!

Todd Fearing, is it? My, my!" he went on, pumping Todd's hand up and down.

"Oh, for pity's sake," murmured Aunt Morbelia. "Come on, boys. I can feel myself growing older as we stand here."

The inside of Harrowwood House was as gray as its outside. Wall hangings that must have been alive with color long ago now hung in pale, dispirited tatters — dust rags rather than works of art. Threadbare strips of grayed carpet lay here and there on the stone floors. Inside it was cold, unlike outside, where it was a sunny summer day.

Aunt Morbelia took hold of the estate agent's arm, propelling him toward the rear of the cavernous entrance hall. "I pray the south wing is in better shape," she said.

"And *warmer*," added Todd, as they went down a wide passageway.

At the end of the passage, they turned left and opened a door that led into the south wing. Here were large rooms filled with heavy old furniture in rose-flowered slipcovers. Reception rooms, Mr. Swallow called them.

"And a modern kitchen," he added, pride in his voice as he ushered them through a swinging door.

Todd's aunt looked from the tiny white enamel refrigerator tucked under a counter, to the blackened stove top, to Mr. Swallow. "What era would you say these appliances are from? *Pre-Christian?*"

A crease appeared on his brow. "Is something wrong?"

Aunt Morbelia drew herself up to her full six feet and glared down at him. "Yes, sir! For thirty years your firm has been drawing monies from the account that accompanies this estate, yet it appears to be on the verge of collapse!"

Because he could barely hear or see her, Mr. Swallow was not intimidated. "But, madam, that account is used to pay the yearly rates! Several thousand pounds last year alone! It pays for upkeep of the lawns . . . glaziers to replace the windows . . ."

Aunt Morbelia tapped him on the shoulder to get his attention. "Your point is well taken. No doubt I am spoilt by living in a modern American house with Todd and his family." The tapping finger became a pat on his shoulder. "And I had forgotten about the taxes — the rates."

"You shall see it all, Miss Fearing, when you examine the accounts with your London solicitor. Mind you, it is very hard to keep up these old manor houses that are haun — er, have a reputation, so to speak. No one will live in."

"Oh, pish, Mr. Swallow. If this estate has a reputation, it is for being in appalling shape."

13

She turned to Todd. "I wonder, would you and Jeff like to check on our rooms now — the bedrooms and bathrooms?"

Glad to leave the dreary kitchen, Todd and Jeff went looking for their rooms. Along with the large reception rooms they found a small library, like a den, well stocked with books. "*Lady of the Lake, The Moonstone, Winnie the Pooh, Dogsbody, Alice in Wonderland, The Strange Case of Dr. Jekyll and Mr. Hyde.*" Jeff was reading across a shelf.

"Oh, good," said Todd, taking *Winnie, Dogsbody,* and *Alice* off the shelf. He had forgotten to pack a book, and yet he had to read something every day if he ever hoped to find reading easy. Determined it would one day be easy, he was a faithful reader.

As he pulled the three books off the shelf, another, smaller book fell forward, giving off a generous puff of dust. Todd picked it up and knocked it against his leg to rid it of more dust. "This one's *The Voyages of Dr. Dolittle,* by Hugh Lofting. Hey, that's one of Dad's favorites. We were going to get it and read it, only we never did."

As he handled the book, a slim, brown volume slipped out of it and fell to the floor. Todd saw the word JOURNAL in faded gold letters on its cover. "Wow. It feels like really soft leather," he said as he picked it up.

Together they examined the slender journal. Writing began on the first yellowed page — spidery, elegant writing that spoke of another time.

For my beloved son, Albert Leatherhead Fearing II, on
the occasion of his Thirty-Fifth Birthday, to be a record of
his time in London. Write and be comforted. Love, Mother.

"This was crazy Cousin Albert's," said Todd, turning the thin pages with care. A quick glance showed
that Albert had filled nearly all the space. Sprinkled
among the journal entries were small sketches that
looked like animal skeletons. Albert was a poor artist,
however, and Todd couldn't tell what they were supposed to be.

"What's that?" Jeff leaned over Todd's shoulder to
stare at some odd designs down the side of one page.

"I haven't the foggiest." Todd studied the facing
page and tried to make out the writing.

Good morning at the Natural History Mueseem. Chap
bear named Farnsworth researching langages as well.
Had lunch together. My progriss slow.

"Geez," muttered Jeff. "Just like the stuff you
write."

"Yeah, he could have been dyslexic, like me."

"And crazy," Jeff added solemnly. "They go together."

"You tired of your teeth? I can fix that, you know."

"Give me a break! Anyway, this guy's not great like
you are. His mistakes are totally boring. Nothing here
is even *close* to *hacky-turctor* or *gaspetti.*"

"Thanks a lot, BB-head," Todd said. He didn't understand why Jeff got such a kick out of those old mistakes, but he always had. "Come on, we'd better find the bedrooms." He slipped the journal into his back pocket, where it fit as if it belonged there. He took *Dr. Dolittle*, too.

They found clean yellow spreads on the beds in two of the six bedrooms. New bars of soap waited on the sinks in those rooms, but the remaining bedrooms were dark and laden with dust. Mattresses pockmarked with holes oozed stuffing wherever mice or rats had set up housekeeping.

"Probably nice and toasty in there," Todd said, nodding at one popular mattress-hotel. "I'll bet this house never gets really warm."

A nearby bathroom with a cracked enamel tub had running water and clean yellow towels on heated towel racks. A separate, tiny room had a toilet, its white ceramic tank mounted high above it on the wall.

"Hey, another kind of toilet," said Todd, tugging on the pull-chain. Train bathrooms, plane bathrooms, old English bathrooms. At last he had a good topic when the next research paper was assigned in school.

When they met up with Aunt Morbelia in the hall, she was surrounded by luggage. Mr. Swallow had gone, and so had the driver of the hire car. "I need my jacket," Todd said.

"Nothing is as cold as a castle or an old stone manor house," agreed his aunt. "Before we start exploring, though, let us take a little rest, all right? Just to recover from jet lag."

As they were getting settled in their rooms, Todd showed her *Dr. Dolittle.*

"Was it Cousin Albert's?" she asked. She opened the book to the title page and read, "*The Voyages of Dr. Dolittle*, by Hugh Lofting, 1922. For Young Albert on his Eighth Birthday, March 1923. Love, Mummy."

"Mummy?" asked Todd.

"Like Mommy in America. What a find, Todd. I should like you to have this book . . . and any others here that you want. We can have the whole lot shipped home, if we wish."

Todd reached for his back pocket. "Here's the best one. His journal."

"It looks like something he would own," she said, gazing down at the thin leather book for a bit before opening it. "May I look at it while we rest?"

"Sure. Check out those strange designs in the back, okay? There're some drawings, too."

The brief rest turned into hours of sleep. When Aunt Morbelia knocked on their door, it was time for dinner.

"Shall we walk into town and inspect the local pub?" she suggested.

Todd squinted at her sleepily. "Isn't a pub a bar?"

"Oh, not at all! Not in the American sense!"

Minutes later they were walking along the narrow, twisting road to Lower Grimsby. "Here is Albert's journal, Todd," said Aunt Morbelia. "I studied those designs you mentioned, but they are nothing I recognize. I wish I did, however. They are quite intriguing."

Todd began leafing through the journal, page by page. "He says here he likes the Tower of London."

"That's supposed to be cool," said Jeff.

Todd was so interested in the journal that Jeff's comment didn't even register. Todd had returned to the pages with the strange markings, which he viewed now as symbols rather than designs. Had Albert gone to London to find out what they meant, or had he learned about them there?

"Why do you think his mom wrote, 'Write and be comforted' on his thirty-fifth birthday?" he asked his aunt.

"Well, that was the year his father died, so I suppose that could be it, although I cannot imagine anyone grieving for that dreadful man for even two minutes!"

"Naughty, naughty," teased Jeff, who had been raised in the house attached to Lorimer's Funeral Parlor. "Dad says we never talk that way about dead people."

"We do about Albert Leatherhead," she replied tartly.

Todd said, "You'd better tell us all about him."

"Yes, but for now, let me explain how to play darts. The pub in Lower Grimsby is famous for darts games."

"Are we real sure it's on this road?" asked Jeff. "We must've gone at least two miles."

"Then we are close," she replied. "My, but I have missed the long summer evenings in England. It will be light until ten, and evening is such a *lovely time* for a walk."

Todd and Jeff exchanged looks. There were walks and there were hikes. Anything over two miles was a hike.

3

The Gamekeeper's Cottage

Much later that evening, as they were getting into their beds, Jeff said, "This was a great day. Man, I loved that darts contest. We have to get a target like that. We could have tournaments and everything!"

At the pub earlier, while they were eating, they had watched a noisy and exciting darts match. They had itched to try throwing darts themselves, but the games lasted until ten-thirty, and then they had begun the trek home.

"After this lovely walk we shall sleep like babies," Aunt Morbelia said. "And by tomorrow we shall be adjusted to British time. Aren't we a clever group though?"

"I'd feel a lot cleverer if we had a car," Todd said.

"*Cars,*" scoffed Aunt Morbelia.

Talk shifted to what they wanted to do in London, and eventually they were back at Harrowwood. The whole day, every minute, had been much more fun than a boring Thursday in Hampshire, Ohio. No wonder people got so excited about vacations, Todd thought as he got into bed.

In the morning, Aunt Morbelia found the kitchen stocked with food and fixed them a "proper English breakfast": fried eggs, grilled tomatoes, bacon, and toast. Then they set out on their inspection tour, across the broad expanse of lawns, toward the acres of old forest.

Inside the forest was another world. Branches of towering oaks arched over shorter trees that had sprung up wherever a shaft of sunlight penetrated. At the sound of footsteps, squirrels skittered to safety on high branches and birds trilled anxious questions back and forth.

Toadstools and leaves, earth and moss had blended their separate smells over time into a fragrance that Todd inhaled with a sudden, strong joy. In only a few steps he felt deep love for the forest. And this perfect place was owned by his aunt . . . and maybe by *him* someday.

"It'd be terrible to sell this," he said.

"I know," Aunt Morbelia replied.

He remembered what she had said about her uncle, Albert Leatherhead. Could there really be murdered bodies lying all around them here in shallow graves? Of course, by now they'd be very old bodies, not fresh corpses like those at Jeff's dad's funeral home. Just bones now, probably. And someday not even bones, because the earth would claim its own again. He had heard that once at a funeral.

"Aunt Morbelia, tell us about Albert Leatherhead. Was he really a murderer? Mr. Swallow started to say Harrowwood was haunted, but he stopped. Did he mean haunted by Albert?"

"I am not sure what he meant, Todd, but I can tell you about my uncle. It is a pretty gruesome tale, though."

"Good," said Jeff.

"Go on," Todd urged. "Creepy stuff doesn't bother me as much as it used to, you know." He gave her his most reassuring smile. Now that he was here, he wanted to know everything about the estate. As a Fearing, this place was part of him. Especially this forest. "Go on," he said again.

"Very well, Todd. Uncle Albert's story begins back in the thirties, when I was about the age you are now. At that time he hired a new gamekeeper — a big, homely man with a bristly, black beard. A silent man. My sisters and I and Cousin Albert were afraid of him at first.

"We all grew to like him, however, as time went

on, especially my cousin. In fact, Cousin Albert and the gamekeeper grew very close, no doubt because they both cared so much about the animals.

"Now as time went on, it appeared that the game-keeper knew what he was doing, and my uncle became famous for the hunts he hosted here on the estate. Uncle Albert's guests bagged more partridge, pheasant, and grouse, more deer and hare, than anywhere else in the south of England. He got a reputation as the owner of a very wealthy estate."

She shook her head disapprovingly. "He became a dreadful braggart. He said that as long as *he* was alive and in charge, his lands would be overflowing with game.

"And yet one day the hunters returned empty-handed from a Harrowwood shoot. They told Albert he must no longer be in charge, as his game had vanished, so he might as well die.

"Well, of course, that infuriated him. He stormed off to the gamekeeper's cottage and when he returned he was covered with mud. No one saw the gamekeeper after that, and not many animals either.

"The forest was abnormally quiet, my cousin wrote. 'Akin to a graveyard' were his exact words. I was in America then, you see, and I am telling you what I learned from Cousin Albert's letters, and from villagers later on.

"Anyway, Uncle Albert began having nightmares. He accused his servants of letting wild creatures into the house after dark. A giant brown hare had been in bed alongside him, he said. Its whiskers had tickled his face.

"The night after that, he woke to find a red deer on either side of his bed, each staring at him with big, sad eyes. The doe said, "Sire, your animals know what you have done, and it is evil. We deserve better. A wise man heeds his animals, Albert Leatherhead." She stomped the floor with her strong hooves, galloped round the bed to join the stag, and both of them leapt out of the open window.

"After that, Albert let it be known he was looking for a new gamekeeper. A pack of wild animals was not going to tell *him* what to do, he told my aunt. 'These are my lands and I shall do as I like!' he told her.

"But that very night, he woke and found his bedroom lit by the full moon, and all around him were his game birds — the pheasants, grouse, and partridge. And sitting on his chest, staring right into his eyes, was an enormous black raven, a bird with a terribly strong beak. It could have pecked out Albert's eyes in a wink, you know.

"This raven had come with a message. 'You are wanted on the morrow in the gamekeeper's cottage,' it said.

"And having said that, the raven flew in a circle round Albert's head and out the window. The other birds followed its path, and one by one they left through the open window.

"Well, once again Albert was in a towering rage. He was convinced someone was deliberately tricking him. Even so, he left home early that day, headed for the forest, and my aunt did not see him again.

"The next morning, thoroughly worried, she went looking for him with the help of servants. They searched through the forest, and finally arrived at the gamekeeper's cottage. There they saw his gun, propped beside the door.

"They threw open the door and Albert lay before them, spread-eagled on the floor. His eyes, engorged with blood, bulged out of his head, and his tongue jutted all black and swollen from his mouth — the face of a hideous death.

"My aunt knelt beside him and saw dozens of marks on his neck, as if he had been strangled by small paws or claws. All about his body and the room were tufts of rabbit hair and birds' feathers and dark pools of dried blood — signs of a fearsome struggle. And in both of Albert's clenched fists were black ravens' feathers."

Aunt Morbelia took a deep breath. "No one knows exactly what happened, of course, but by this time my aunt had a pretty fair idea of what had been going on. In searching the forest, she and the servants had found many empty cages and pens, all cunningly hidden. She felt sure Albert had caged the game until time for a shoot, and then had directed his gamekeeper to turn them all loose in the area of the hunt.

"It was a vicious system, of course. The penned creatures could not run or fly like normal ones and were easy pickings. No wonder men loved a shoot at Harrowwood.

"Afterwards, local people began saying that the ghosts of the dead animals had feared my uncle planned to fill the cages again so the hunts would go on as before, until he died. And so, the animals made sure that he died," she concluded, matter-of-factly.

Todd frowned in concentration. "But the gamekeeper? Did he go somewhere, or did Uncle Albert kill him?"

"I think Uncle Albert murdered the poor fellow. My guess is that the gamekeeper reached a point when he could no longer bear to do what my uncle told him. He could no longer ignore his conscience, and so he revolted. Turned all the animals and birds loose. Emptied every hateful pen on the estate.

"That would explain why the hunters found no game that day, and why the forest was so silent and empty of animals for a time. I think they fled until they felt it was safe to return. And remember, no one ever saw the gamekeeper after the day that my uncle went off in a rage to his cottage."

"Plenty of reasons for the animals to hate Albert Leatherhead," Jeff observed.

"The skeleton in our family closet," said Todd.

"My, yes. I remember feeling so sorry for Cousin Albert at the time. Learning what his father had done . . . having his wonderful gamekeeper friend disappear with no trace . . . well, I think it pushed him over the edge. So when I say that no one mourned the death of Albert Leatherhead, now you know why."

At this point in their walk, a clearing opened out ahead of them, and there was the gamekeeper's cottage. Sun shone down on the deteriorating thatch, where birds had nested year after year.

Aunt Morbelia walked up to the front door and raised its latch. "I know it will be awful inside, but I love this place. My sisters and I used to come here with Cousin Albert, to get away from the adults.

"Ophelia told ghost stories, and Albert would make the most wonderful, spooky sounds to go along, so that we were all petrified. It was simply grand," she finished, her voice soft with memory.

Hmm, thought Todd, following her into the cottage. No wonder she likes ghosts. She grew up with them.

"Not as bad in here as I feared," she said after a quick look around. "I expect local people come in occasionally."

Todd said, "At least we know it isn't hunters — unless people still poach game." But it wouldn't be very comfortable here, he thought. There was no furniture and the filthy windows barely let in any light. Dirt and leaves covered the stone floor, so that every step sounded as if they were still walking in the forest.

"Great place for a camp-out," Jeff said, looking around. "What's that?" He pointed to an overhead door.

"A loft for the gamekeeper's traps," Aunt Morbelia replied. "The adults were afraid that a child might fiddle with one and be maimed or killed. Animal traps were always kept far away from children. I have never been up there."

"Can't you just see this place all fixed up?" Jeff went on. "With bunks, I mean? It'd make an awesome camp."

"Oh, yes," Aunt Morbelia agreed eagerly. "We were allowed to do that sometimes. Cousin Albert arranged it. We came in a pony cart, with a picnic and coverlets, and it was such fun. Cordelia used to imitate Albert Leatherhead, and we would nearly die laughing. I shall never forget it. Cousin Albert said she was good enough to go on the stage, but of course, a lady did not do that in those days."

The more Todd heard about Cousin Albert, the

more he wished he had known him. Having the journal made him seem even more real. "Aunt Morbelia," he said, "you read the journal. Wouldn't it be cool if we could figure out what he meant with those symbols?"

The corners of her mouth went up slightly. "And how would we do that? Somehow I feel sure you have an idea."

"Yeah, I do! Let's go to London and do what Albert did! We don't have a plan anyway. I mean, we always said we'd do what looked interesting." Todd pulled the journal from his back pocket. "Well, this looks interesting — like a puzzle. See how carefully he made these symbols here in the back? They just have to mean something important."

"Whoops, we're losing him, Aunt M," cried Jeff. "He's going over the edge."

"It would seem so," she said, peering at Todd over her spectacles, pretending to be a disapproving teacher.

But she said "Yes" right away. "Wouldn't we feel smart if we did find the answer? Goodness! You had better pack the *Dolittle* book, too, Todd. Just in case. After all, you found them hidden together."

Todd felt a rush of excitement. "Good idea. Do you think we ought to search Harrowwood, or maybe right here?" He stopped. "Of course, I don't know what we're looking for."

Jeff considered the bleak little room, decorated

only with the grime of decades. "Probably hopeless," he agreed, "but I still think it'd make a great camp."

"No reason why not," said Aunt Morbelia. "Maybe you and Todd could set up a camp here someday. Students love to live and study in other countries. Jeff, you be sure to spend time abroad when you are in college. A semester, perhaps."

Jeff shook his head. "Dad's groaning about tuition for four kids now. He'd never pay for a semester abroad."

"Then I shall have to talk to him," she replied. "I know lots of ways you can study abroad for the same cost. And in the summer you can bike and camp out, or live in youth hostels. Or, as you said, right here in this cottage."

They talked, and Todd wandered around wishing they were outside in the forest. He kicked up a flutter of leaves. What he saw beneath them caused him to stop and kneel down.

As Aunt Morbelia and Jeff, still talking, headed toward the door, Todd rubbed the dark spot with his finger. He worked the slippery substance between his finger and thumb and sniffed it. Then he looked overhead at the trapdoor.

Thoughtfully, he put his hand in his pocket to guard the bit of moisture on his fingers. He strolled over to the fireplace and poked through the leaves.

Leaves? Why were leaves piled in a fire grate? Why so many ashes under the leaves?

I'm getting a bad feeling in here, he decided, turning away from the fireplace. "Coming," he called to the others, who were waiting outside the door.

As he left, Todd looked up at the trapdoor again. Its broad brass hinges bore all the dirt and rust of half a century, but where the metal parts meshed, they gleamed.

Someone had opened that door recently. He wondered if anyone was up there now, listening. Watching them through cracks in the old wooden boards of the loft.

4

Sounds in the Night

After seeing about half the estate, they went back to the house. As soon as they were alone, Todd stuck the fingers he'd been guarding under Jeff's nose. "What do you think it is?"

Jeff inhaled, wiggling his nose like a thoughtful beagle. "I'm guessing oil or grease — stuff Dad uses when he works on our hearse." Mr. Lorimer did all the repairs himself on the gleaming, antique hearse, which was a feature attraction of their family funeral business.

"Just guess where it was," Todd said, rushing on. "Right under the trapdoor! And those *hinges are shiny.* What'd you bet somebody's using that loft? They could have been up there listening to us!"

That idea made them both quiet and thoughtful during lunch. They went back outside eagerly, needing to be distracted, and by late Friday afternoon, they'd seen the rest of the estate — all of the forest as well as the many neglected fields bordered by stout green hedges. No place had ever appealed to Todd like the forest.

As they walked, he and Jeff thought of a few people who might be using the old cottage: those without homes, perhaps, or modern-day poachers. The loft was a perfect hideaway. No doubt there was a logical explanation that had nothing sinister about it, and they could quit worrying.

As they cleaned up to go to dinner, Todd said, "Let's come back here when we're done sightseeing, okay?"

"Fine by me. I don't care what we do. I'm just glad I'm not home mowing lawns."

They grabbed jackets on the way out of their room, as Aunt Morbelia had warned them about a chilly evening in the country. "I can't believe we're walking to another town after walking all day long," Jeff said.

"Sorry, but Aunt Morbelia *loves* walking."

"I know. Remember when she first moved in with your family and we took her on a big walk to see the caves and the lake and the real old houses, and she fainted in our funeral parlor when that corpse went by? Remember that?"

"Sure! Your dad wanted to cremate us." By now, of course, that heart-stopping episode in the funeral parlor had become funny. Amazing, Todd thought, how time could improve on a bad experience.

Aunt Morbelia met them in the courtyard again, but this evening she took them to a bus stop. Twenty minutes later, they stepped off the bus on High Street in Oxblood.

"It is still here!" Aunt Morbelia was pointing to a low, Tudor inn with a weathered sign that creaked back and forth in the breeze. "The Snooty Fox" it said, above a prancing fox wearing a tuxedo and a haughty look.

Inside, she glanced swiftly around before turning to them and smiling. "I simply love it when good things do not change. See over there? Darts. And the public is allowed to use them. Go on. I shall coach from the bench."

Todd went first and held his dart exactly as she showed him. He aimed, drew his arm back, never took his eye off the round, bristle-board target, and let fly. The dart sank into the wall to the left of the target.

His second dart hit a wire divider on the target, bounced off, and crashed to the floor. His third dart hit the wall on the right, and that ended his turn.

Jeff stood up. "Well, here goes the old ego."

Much later they were creeping, hard-won point by hard-won point, down toward zero and the end of their first game. They played a second game, which went a bit faster, before sitting down to a dinner of roast "baby chicken" with creamed potatoes and vegetables. Aunt Morbelia was practically purring.

Todd said, "Calling it 'baby chicken' makes me feel like an assassin."

Aunt Morbelia chewed reflectively before answering. "I think the British still call a nettle a nettle, as the saying goes. For example, a person with epilepsy here has *fits*, but Americans call them *seizures* — a much less negative word."

By the time the meal was over, both Todd and Jeff were yawning, and at the end of the ride home they stumbled, half asleep, down the bus steps. In their room, they wasted no time getting into bed.

Once in bed, however, Todd's imagination drew disturbingly clear pictures of Albert Leatherhead's murder. He opened his eyes, needing to reassure himself that nothing was amiss, and there was the moon, streaming through the tall windows into their room. Oh, poop, he thought, slipping out of bed, wincing as his feet touched the icy floor.

He tugged on the window latches to be sure they were securely fastened. Nothing was going to get in here if he could help it. Probably dumb old Albert Leatherhead had slept with his windows open for some nice, fresh, thirty-degree air.

"I already checked those windows," Jeff said.

*   *   *

When Todd woke around four, he checked his watch, wondering why he was awake in the dark. I heard something, he decided, listening for sounds from Jeff's bed.

"Hey, Todd?"

"Hey yourself. Did you make some kind of noise?"

"No, but I heard a really weird one."

"How weird? *Bad* weird?"

"Pretty bad, yeah. We could maybe hear it better out in the hall."

Todd hesitated a second, then flung back his covers. They hopped across the chilly flagstones, out the door, and over to the thin carpet runner in the hall. There they stood and shivered and listened.

Nothing. For a long time, nothing.

"Just think about winter here," Jeff whispered.

"I know. My hair's got frostbite already." Then Todd went rigid.

From somewhere far away came a sound he had never heard before — an eerie, unearthly moaning. He could feel his feet freezing on the icy floor of the hall, but he couldn't make them move.

The moan rose slightly, then fell to guttural depths. It went on and on, rising and falling, until Todd wanted to scream. Was it somebody in terrible pain? Could a wounded animal be nearby? At last the moan dwindled to a whimper, and finally there was only silence.

"What makes a sound like *that?*" whispered Jeff.

"Who knows?" Todd wrapped his arms around his body to stop his shivering. Even his teeth were chattering, something he thought happened only in books.

He glanced down the hall to his aunt's room, hoping she had heard the sounds and would come charging out, armed with her umbrella. But her door stayed shut. Enough of this, he thought, jogging determinedly back to the warmth of his bed.

From the doorway Jeff said, "What're you doing?"

"Bringing my body temperature up above freezing. What does it look like?"

"It looks like chickening out!"

"Chickening out of what?"

"Going to find out what made that noise! We have to find out!"

"Oh yeah? Why?" asked Todd, buying time. Jeff had always been this way, like Rikki Tikki Tavi the mongoose. Their shared motto was "Run and find out," whereas Todd's was "Go slowly and figure it out."

Maybe it's because I'm dyslexic, he thought. I mess up when I go too fast.

By now, Jeff was back in his bed and talking: ". . . probably normal, well, not exactly normal, but something we don't know about because we don't live here. Maybe a wolf in the woods . . . or people using the estate — the loft people, you know? We should go find them *right now*."

Todd closed his eyes. He wasn't sure he wanted to find anything that could make such a horrible sound. At least not until daylight. And he wished he had Inky. There was no substitute for a big, strong dog.

At last he said, "We ought to think about this. I mean, what if it's a wild animal right here in the house? And we come up on him in the dark?"

"In the house?" Jeff's voice rose. "How would a wild animal get in here?"

"I don't know! But we saw ravens fly out of the tower! Maybe the other side of the house is a total wreck. We haven't even been over there."

Jeff groaned. "So let's go now!

Any longer and he'll call me a chicken again, Todd thought. "Okay, okay, but I'm not going in my underwear."

"So take it off, but let's go!"

Har har, Todd thought, grimly rooting for a sweatshirt in his suitcase. Jeff put on warm clothes, too, and with the flashlight his mom had insisted on packing, they set off through the cold, dark hallways.

Just to be thorough, they searched their own area first, although no one would use rooms so close, they reasoned. In the four reception rooms and the remaining four bedrooms they saw lacy spiderwebs — each an intricate delicacy illuminated by their light. Now and then the flashlight shone on mice, which fled squeaking in terror.

In time they were inching down the black, empty passageway toward the main entrance hall. Todd couldn't help but worry about the other wing of the house. Ignored for over a hundred years, it could be dangerous. Criminals could be living in its many rooms. Rotting floors might drop away beneath them. Rats could gnaw on their ankles.

In the entrance hall, he stood by the front door and peered out the long, dirty windows at the courtyard. Rain was falling from a sky the color of coal. Even when day arrived, it would be gray and dreary.

And then they heard it again: piercing cries this time that only gradually slipped into the eerie moaning they had heard earlier.

"It's over there, and above us," Jeff whispered, waving his hand at the north wing. "Maybe up where the ravens flew out of the tower. Hey, you know, that could be it — just some dumb old birds messing around."

That's lame, Todd thought, but he said, "Right. So let's go back to bed. Can't see a thing at night."

"Look, whatever it is, it's there *right now*. Come on!"

Jeff's voice sounded some distance away, on the

opposite side of the hall, and Todd went in that direction. "Yeah, but don't you think — "

Jeff grabbed hold of Todd's shirt and pulled him into a passageway that seemed exactly like the one they'd just come through, the one from the south wing to the entrance hall. Reassured by its familiarity, Todd thought, oh, all right. The north wing will be just like the south wing, no big deal. Besides that, it was easier just to humor Jeff when he got into one of these determined moods.

Jeff shone the flaring beam of his flashlight on a wide oak staircase. Step by step, the old wood creaking under their feet, they tiptoed upward. Across a broad landing. Up another, more decrepit staircase to the second story.

Todd whispered, "This place is huge. What're we going to do if we find somebody? Point a finger and say 'Don't move or I'll shoot?' Or maybe call the cops?"

Jeff stopped. "We don't have a phone, do we?"

"Nope."

"Well, let's see if we can figure out — "

A series of cries erupted around them — much, much closer — echoing eerily through the hallways and empty rooms. The half-human, half-animal screeches nailed both of them to the floor, rendering them stiff with horror.

Whatever it was, it sounded insane. One wild, tormented cry erupted after another in seemingly endless agony.

Todd gripped Jeff's arm and felt his friend's clammy flesh. In the cold of this stone-cold house, Jeff was pouring sweat, and Todd knew he wasn't the only one who was scared.

The cries ceased, and in their place was a long, heavy minute of silence. Then the low moaning resumed, rising and falling in its awful rhythm. Todd's imagination raced. Were these the wails of crazy people?

Somehow he found the banister at the top of the staircase. "I'm gone," he whispered.

"Hurry!" breathed Jeff.

Side by side, following the jiggling beam of the flashlight, they fled down the stairs, across the landing, and down again, tearing along the passageway toward the entrance hall, crashing through the door into the hall, uncaring of any noise, desperate to get away from those fiendish cries. They ran across the entrance hall, down the black passageway toward the south wing, and finally into their own area of the house, and Todd was still holding his breath.

Back in their room, Todd shut the door and forced the old bolt to slide into place. Safe at last, he could breathe now — deep, rasping, grateful breaths of air.

Just then Jeff gave a strange cry and grabbed Todd's arm. Todd looked across the room to where Jeff was pointing and saw the ragged, tan draperies fluttering in the breeze from the open windows.

When they'd left, only minutes before, those windows had been shut and locked.

5

The Open Windows

In shock, Todd stared across their bedroom at the open windows. When he was at last able to talk, he whispered, "Flashlight."

Jeff sent a jittery beam of light around the room. He knelt down and shone the light under the beds, too, and then opened the tall wardrobe. All the hiding places were empty.

Feeling better, Todd said, "Suitcases."

Jeff aimed the light, steadier now, across the tops of their suitcases, open on the floor. "It was kind of a mess to begin with, so I can't tell if somebody's been in my stuff or not," he said.

"Mine, too." Todd pressed the light button on his watch. It was four-thirty, and heavy rain and clouds kept the sky dark. For now, he locked the windows again and pulled the draperies before getting back into bed.

Irritably he said to Jeff, "We won't even be able to check for footprints if this dopey rain doesn't let up."

"Why would anybody come in here? We hardly have any money, and I didn't bring anything valuable. Did you?"

"I don't even *own* anything valuable, except my new camera, and it's on the dresser where I left it. I checked that right away. Do you think they got our windows open from the outside somehow? Or maybe came from somewhere inside the house, and left by the windows when they heard us coming?"

"We were pretty noisy, running and all. I'll bet they heard us and split. Just zoop, out the window," said Jeff.

"Yeah, but that means they were *in the house*." A really bad thought, he decided, folding his pillow in half to prop his head up. "Aunt Morbelia must be right, and ravens are bad luck." Then he laughed. "But that's dumb. Birds don't know what they're doing. A bird's got a brain the size of a pea."

"That means *girl* here," Jeff said, changing the subject.

"What?"

"*Bird* is slang here for *girl*. I heard it in a movie we rented once. And my brothers call girls *chicks* . . . so I guess girls are poultry everywhere."

"What are guys?"

"I don't know. I sort of like *hunk,* myself. We can just be hunks, okay?"

"Sounds good to me." Todd vaulted out of bed. "Let's pack and get it over with. This is *some house,* boy. I think it'd be *easy* to go crazy here!"

The stubborn rain was still falling at nine when the hire car and the same silent driver arrived to take them to London. As the car left the driveway and turned onto the road, Todd gazed out the window at the forest.

In those woods lived all kinds of birds he had never seen before . . . fat, sassy squirrels . . . millions of bugs and spiders . . . and the graceful, big-eared, big-eyed hare that nested in nearby fields and made flying leaps across the paths in front of him. Deer, too, and — heck, I could spend years there, he thought.

"You appear sorry to be leaving," said his aunt.

"Can we come back before we go home? I really like the forest."

"I do, too, Todd. That is the true beauty of the place, of course. The house is rather a nightmare."

"That's for sure!" Jeff gave Todd a meaningful look.

"Right," he said. "Aunt Morbelia, did you hear anything last night?"

"No. Well, I heard wind — quite late — and sounds from the woods. Animals, I suppose. Why do you ask?"

"Because Jeff and I heard some weird moaning noises somewhere over in the north wing. Up on the second floor. We went to check, but . . . ." Todd's voice faded as Aunt Morbelia turned her dark, penetrating eyes on him. If he hadn't known her well, he'd have been really scared. She could melt a guy down to a little pile of bones and hair, he thought, just by looking at him.

"You went wandering through the house in the night?" she asked. "In the dark?"

"Yes, but we had a flashlight and we thought we ought to check it out. They were horrible noises."

"*Very, very* horrible," added Jeff.

"Well, I wish I had heard them."

"No way. It was maximum creepy," Todd said.

Her eyes widened with interest. "How fascinating! If something like that happens again, you be sure to wake me."

"Okay. But anyhow, when we got back to our room, our windows were open . . . and we locked them the night before. They were locked for sure. So somebody was in our room when we weren't there! Somebody must be on the estate . . . somewhere . . . because they opened our windows!"

Aunt Morbelia frowned. "That settles it. We must have a new estate agent. That is, if we keep Harrowwood. Nice as he may be, Mr. Swallow is no longer fit for the job. He would not know whether squatters had moved in or not — and they do move into unoccupied houses all over the U.K., or so I have been told."

Feeling eyes upon them, Todd gave the driver's rearview mirror a peek. Yup. This time the man was not only staring, he was obviously listening to their conversation.

What a snoop, Todd decided. With his hands below the seat, where the driver couldn't see, Todd pointed to him and made a cross-out, nix-this sign to his aunt.

Her eyes flicked up to the rearview mirror and back to Todd, and she gave him a tiny nod. "Let me tell you about some of the things in London that I think you two would enjoy," she began.

Before she had a chance, Todd said, "Okay, but remember how we talked about going where Cousin Albert went?" He eased the journal out of his back pocket.

"We can do that, Todd, but I hate to see you get your hopes up about discovering some hidden meaning in those little symbols or drawings. They could have been just doodles, when he was thinking of something else, or designs he found interesting. Cousin Albert was more than a trifle eccentric, you know."

Their car swerved, nearly running off the road, and Aunt Morbelia spoke sharply. "I say up there! Do watch where you are going! The traffic is quite heavy here."

The driver mumbled a reply, which Todd couldn't understand. Apparently neither could his aunt, who was shaking her head in exasperation.

"Remember this part?" He showed her one of the earlier pages in the journal.

" 'Very meeningful day in the Naturel History Muesem,' " she read. "Hmm, *meaningful*. I remember thinking that was an interesting choice of word." She pointed to a group of sketches. "And this is almost like an anatomy lesson, but I cannot recall his ever being interested in anatomy."

In the rearview mirror, Todd saw the driver's eyes again. Strange, spooky eyes — much too inquisitive, and given to staring. A total creep, Todd thought.

"Very well, Natural History it is, then," said Aunt Morbelia. "I must say my curiosity is growing, as it always did whenever I was around Albert. Such a dear, strange person . . . although a poor speller."

Todd looked out the window to hide a grin. She would always be a teacher, no matter what.

In spite of London's clogged streets, they were settled at their bed-and-breakfast by noon. Ye Olde Saxon Inne was run by friends of the Fearing family.

As they walked toward a fish-and-chips shop for lunch, Aunt Morbelia said, "I fear I have trespassed on an old friendship. From the notices posted in our rooms, I see that Major and Mrs. Dwiddle could be making twice what they're charging us, yet they would not hear of our staying elsewhere."

"We'll be real nice to them," Todd promised.

They ate quickly, enjoying the fresh, crispy codfish and potatoes, which were served in nests of newspaper. Lunch over, they set out for the Natural History Museum, only a few blocks down Cromwell Street.

"It's huge!" said Jeff as they came within sight of the museum and its tall tower.

"Four acres of exhibits — or thereabouts," Aunt Morbelia said. "We could spend a week in here."

Todd began to question his idea of following in Albert's footsteps. At home, his parents and Jeff's regularly dragged them through museums. He and Jeff had not come to England to spend three weeks in *museums*. No way.

I'd better take charge here, he thought. "Let's find somebody in zoology," he said, marching resolutely past a lifelike model of a blue whale.

"It is ninety-one feet long," Aunt Morbelia announced.

"Biggest mammal on earth," Jeff added, knowing how she loved to hear kids say things like that.

As they walked the long museum halls, Todd became aware of a noisy tapping right behind them. He looked back over his shoulder and got a glimpse of a young woman in black — lots of black that billowed all around her — with blood-red scarves draped around her neck and shoulders. Her shoes were black, teetery high heels — the tallest shoes he had ever seen. And she wore black-rimmed, thick glasses and a dorky hat.

"Why do girls wear those dumb shoes?" he whispered to Jeff.

"Nobody knows," Jeff whispered back. "Get a load of her outfit. That hat looks like a squashed purple cabbage. What'd you bet she's some kind of actress?"

They waited while Aunt Morbelia spoke to a guard. Then she pointed to the end of the gallery, where a woman was locking an exhibit case. "Todd, you may ask questions of her. She is one of the curators here."

She looks really smart, he thought, walking quickly toward the curator, a middle-aged woman with a heavy braid wound round her head. He hoped she could take one look at Cousin Albert's drawings and know what he had been trying to depict.

Todd introduced himself and explained briefly about the journal. "He was here when he drew these pictures. And maybe these symbols. Do they mean anything to you?"

Tap, tap, tap, tap. That girl in the noisy heels was only inches away, looking at the specimens in the display case where the curator had recently been working.

Todd put himself between her and the curator, who was examining the journal. She looked up from it and smiled at him, her blue eyes direct and friendly.

Shaking her head she said, "I can't help you, I'm afraid. However, I can photocopy some pages, if you like, and show them to various members of our staff. We have excellent ornithologists, of course, and these appear to be bird skeletons.

"Or perhaps . . ." She squinted at another drawing. "Perhaps a rabbit or a squirrel. We'll have a look, all of us, and I can send a note to your hotel if we get something definite."

"These symbols? And these? Have you seen anything like them before?"

"I'm sorry, but I really don't think so. I'll just nip down to my office and make copies."

Todd turned and nearly bumped into the girl in black, who was standing right in his path, close enough to have been eavesdropping. She gave him a peculiar look and teetered off to a distant display case.

Sheesh, he thought. First the hire car driver, now her. People in England must think we have a funny accent or something, he decided, as he rejoined his aunt and Jeff.

"So how'd it go?" said Jeff.

"Too soon to tell. She's making copies and she'll call us if anybody here recognizes anything. It's okay," he said, determinedly optimistic. "We just got started."

When the curator returned, they wrote down the address of Ye Olde Saxon Inne. "The proprietors are good friends," Aunt Morbelia told the woman. "They will pass on any message, and we are very grateful for your assistance."

"You're most welcome. Dare I ask what you're researching?"

Todd thought a bit and said, "I don't know. But I think it'll be cool if we ever figure it out."

After many exhibits of dinosaur skeletons, bugs, and animals — all more interesting than Todd had expected — they left the museum. Out on the sidewalk he said, "I didn't see a thing in there that was in the journal. How about you guys?"

"No," said his aunt, "but it is early days yet, as you pointed out before. We shall go enjoy tea, how about that?"

"Aunt Morbelia, do you think it's dumb to try to figure out that stuff in the journal? See, it's just a hunch — "

She held up her hand, a commanding gesture. "Ah, but a strong one, Todd, I can tell. That is called intuition, a kind of second sight. Intuition is responsible for many of the greatest discoveries and inventions in the world."

Jeff gave Todd a hefty thump on the back. "It's just like being a bloodhound. You follow your nose."

6

A Nasty Look

As they walked toward his aunt's favorite tea shop, Todd listened not to her talk with Jeff, but to what was behind them — that same noisy tapping from the museum. It made no sense, as he had been telling himself for the last couple hours, but that girl seemed to be following them. By now he hated her and her stupid shoes.

He elbowed Jeff and whispered, "Don't turn around. We're being followed."

Jeff stared straight ahead. "Who?"

"That girl in the weird clothes."

Jeff began to grin. "Yeah, you're a hunk all right, but she's not after *us*. We're not old enough."

"You twink! That's not why she's doing it!"

"So why is she?"

"How should *I* know? Have you ever seen her before?"

"Of course not . . . but you're right, she's been with us a pretty long time."

"You bet she has."

Aunt Morbelia had stopped to admire some flowers, but now she caught up with them. "The shop is just up there on the left. Emma Dwiddle says it is still outstanding."

They entered the small, noisy tea shop and chose a booth in the front bay window, at Todd's suggestion. He was curious to see if the girl would follow them in.

While his aunt spoke to the waitress, Todd leaned forward in the window and looked out to the sidewalk, first right, then left. Sure enough. Nose in the air, eyes straight ahead, there she came. He watched as she tapped her way regally past the window, her black garments and red scarves streaming behind her. Like a pirate ship, he thought.

Under his breath he said, "Toodle-oo, Sweetie." But just as he mouthed the words, she whipped her head around and looked him squarely in the eyes. It was a fierce, calculated look. Icy as the floors in Harrowwood House. Then she faced forward again, moving swiftly away.

Todd sank back against his seat. How had she known he was watching? She acted as if she wanted him to see her.

"Todd, is something wrong?" Aunt Morbelia reached across the table and put her hand on his.

"Uh . . . nothing . . ."

"He's got a headache, Aunt M," Jeff said. "Come on. Let's check out the loo and you can take an aspirin. Mom made me bring this," he explained, red-faced, as he produced a square pillbox from his pocket.

In the men's room, Todd said, "Good thinking. I didn't know what to say."

"What happened? You looked kind of sick."

"That girl gave me a look that'd make *anybody* sick. She's got some kind of problem, that's for sure."

"Maybe we did something wrong that we don't even know about. You could ask Aunt M," Jeff suggested.

What Todd's aunt referred to as "a proper tea" was on the table when they returned. "Hey, look at that!" crowed Jeff, who was hungry twenty-four hours a day.

"How do you feel, Todd?" Aunt Morbelia asked.

"Okay. Maybe it's jet lag. Dad says it takes him a week to feel normal in a different time zone." He glanced at the loaded table. "This isn't *tea*. This is awesome."

While he and Jeff devoured one elegant sandwich after another, Todd asked his aunt about the strange girl in the museum. "She just went by here," he said. "She turned around and gave me this real mean look, too.

Why do you think she did that?" He helped himself to another smoked salmon triangle.

"I have no idea, although I do recall that young woman," said Aunt Morbelia, dabbing her mouth with her napkin. "If you were staring at her all afternoon, I imagine she is somewhat annoyed by now. I should forget her if I were you."

Todd nearly choked on his sandwich. "I didn't stare at her! She stared at *me!* She went everywhere *I* did!"

Gently Aunt Morbelia said, "Todd, dear, you described every inch of that young woman to me, even down to how tall her heels were. You have never taken that much notice of a human being before, so I assume you found her very interesting. That is perfectly normal! But she may not have taken your interest as a compliment, and took offense instead."

Todd stuffed a lemon tart in his mouth. "Right," he growled, looking down at the table. She had missed his meaning entirely.

A dainty blue square of cake, decorated with tiny flowers and riding on the palm of Jeff's hand, appeared under his nose. "Try one," said Jeff. "They're great. Chocolate inside." And he knew that what Jeff meant was, *hang in there. We'll talk later.*

"Thanks," he said, licking off one pink flower.

Much later he said, "Oink. Any more and I'll pop."

"You really know food, Aunt M," added Jeff.

"Boys are so satisfactory to feed," she said, smiling, as she got up to pay their bill.

Todd consulted the journal. "Cousin Albert spent a lot of time in Hyde Park. Outdoors. That sounds good, Jeff, don't you think?"

"Yup. Let's go for it."

As they left the tea shop, Aunt Morbelia said, "Oh, look, it has stopped raining. We shall walk. London was made for walking."

They went slowly, enjoying everything that wasn't at all like their own small town in southern Ohio. Double-decker buses, manicured hedges, mini cars that were truly mini, and black, capacious taxicabs. "We shall definitely take some cab rides," Aunt Morbelia said, pointing out a particularly ancient-looking cab with an antiquated driver to match.

Yet all the while Todd listened for those unnerving high heels. After a time he concluded two things: she was nowhere around and he had the world's biggest imagination. Why, he wondered, do I always imagine the worst?

Sunday morning they walked with the Dwiddles to their church. "Miraculously spared in the Great Fire of 1666," Mrs. Dwiddle told them.

"And we've got a bloody good choir!" boomed

Major Dwiddle, a stout, red-faced man of seventy. "Bloody good choir!" he repeated, his bushy white eyebrows leaping upward, as they often did when he spoke.

His wife and Aunt Morbelia sucked in their breath and tutted together. "Duncan, really," scolded little Mrs. Dwiddle. "We are practically on the church steps and you're swearing!" Her white curls quivered.

Hmm, thought Todd, mentally filing the Major's word away for later use. No one in America would consider *bloody* a bad word. He could say it anytime he felt like it. Given the strange things that had happened to them so far on this trip, he guessed he might feel like it before long.

After church, they had Sunday lunch with the Dwiddles. "No trouble at all," Emma Dwiddle insisted when Todd's aunt protested. "The Major's brother, Farley, is coming and it'll be just like a party."

And so they all sat down to a fragrant beef roast accompanied by vast heaps of boiled vegetables. "Mmmhmm," said the Major's brother, a robust man in his mid sixties. "Nothing like this in the Army, nossir. Now, folks, whilst I do justice to this food, you can tell me what I'm going to do with myself. I've been retired one week and already I'm bored out of my skull!" He gave a hearty laugh and picked up his fork.

Major Dwiddle started in on the pleasures of

gardening, and Todd took a bite of vegetables. They went instantly to mush in his mouth, but although he chewed a piece of the beef until his jaws ached, it remained tough and resilient and *there*. It's growing, he thought, revolted by the meaty wad.

At home, he'd have taken it out of his mouth and looked at it, no matter what his folks said. He might even have mounted it on a poster as an exhibit, since he'd never known a piece of meat to behave this way.

But because he was a guest in someone's home, at a special meal, and in a foreign country, he swallowed the lump and let it make its slow, painful way down his throat. The rest of his meat he buried under some cabbage.

For dessert he had two helpings of raspberry trifle, as did the Major's brother. "I'll do up the kitchen," Farley offered. The Major and his wife didn't argue, but went upstairs for "a little lie-down," as the Major put it.

"Naps are a waste of time," said Aunt Morbelia, heading for the front hall. "Well, Todd, where does Cousin Albert suggest we go today?"

"Hyde Park," he said, fishing the journal out of his pocket. "He spent a lot of time there."

7

A Question in Hyde Park

"There it is," said Aunt Morbelia, pointing with her umbrella. "Gloucester Road Station, right where I left it."

Todd sounded out the letters on the sign: *glow-you-sess-ter.* But she had said *gloster,* to rhyme with *foster.*

Suddenly he felt her hand on his shoulder. "Remember Worcestershire sauce that sounds like *wuhs-teh-sheer?* Sometimes sounding it out just does not help, I am afraid."

Inside the station they stood in front of a large, colorful map. Aunt Morbelia said, "You can see the route of each subway train. Once you know the system, you may go wherever you want."

Using her umbrella as a schoolroom pointer, she said, "See? Here is where we are, and right there is Marble Arch, the main entrance to the park. Take your time and plan our route. Then buy our fares and meet me over at that bench."

Todd felt his mind seize up. He had never even looked at the money she'd given him when they arrived, nor had he ridden a subway. And all these strange spellings. Well, he just couldn't do it.

Seeing his expression, Aunt Morbelia said, "Study the map first, then the fare chart. Every pound has one hundred pence, just like one hundred pennies to the dollar. You will be able to work it out." With that, she went to the bench, where she propped her black umbrella and sat down to look over some papers her solicitor had sent. Todd saw her brow crease in concentration before he turned away.

With Jeff, he stared at the map.

"Well, she's not lecturing us," Jeff said.

"Now would be okay!"

But a brief study of the map soon proved she was right, and they could figure it out. From their station on the yellow Circle Line, they could transfer to any other line and go wherever they wanted, even to Heathrow airport. With his finger, Todd traced their route. No sweat.

"I'll get the tickets," he said, his confidence growing.

The London subway was old, but highly efficient. It racketed along under the city, making brief stops, and in a few minutes they were in Notting Hill Gate Station, where they switched to the red Central Line. A few stops later, they were at Marble Arch Station. Just like that. Todd felt as if he had conquered the city.

At the entrance to the park, Aunt Morbelia paused near the Marble Arch. Swooping her umbrella in a wide circle, she said, "This area was called Tyburn in medieval days. It was a good site for public executions because of its central location and size."

"Did they want a big crowd?" asked Todd.

"My, yes. Hangings and beheadings were very popular. Also, executing criminals in public was supposed to convince people not to commit crimes. It did not work, of course."

In the background, they could hear shouting mixed with clapping. Aunt Morbelia said, "Come along. That fellow is drawing quite a crowd."

In nearby Speaker's Corner, a tall, freckled man with only a few wisps of red hair was explaining The Joys of Vegetarianism. He promised them regular bowel movements and thick, luxuriant heads of hair if they would just eat brussels sprouts every day.

One man in the crowd yelled, "Better follow your own advice, mate!" A chubby woman in a pink sweatsuit held up a small, wire-haired terrier and pointed it at the speaker as if it were a weapon. The terrier barked shrilly and didn't stop until the vegetarian gave up and quit talking.

The next speaker was a thin woman, with limp, walnut-colored hair that obscured her face. Dressed entirely in green, she explained what it was like to be a tree. "And then come the winds of winter, and the cold, chill rains, the lashing of an icy storm," she cried, swaying wildly back and forth in her own storm.

"How about a nice walk?" Todd said, somehow sure that Speaker's Corner was not what had lured Cousin Albert to the park. I wonder why he hung out here so much, Todd thought, remembering that Hyde Park appeared several places in the journal.

As they walked beside a small lake, he leafed through an early section of the journal. In Cousin Albert's tiny, precise script he read,

> *All day at Hyde Park. Much food*
> *for thoght bear. A truely grand*
> *convocation of the world's speeces. (sp?)*
> *And I am their Ancient Marriner,*
> *an albatross round my neck.*
>
> *New today: aa ⓐ ⓐ ⓐ uuu aa*

Todd stared at the distinctive little symbols, appearing here for the first time. They looked similar to the other symbols arrayed in tidy columns at the back of the journal.

He handed the journal to his aunt. "See what he wrote when he was here? Funny little drawings, too."

Aunt Morbelia looked at the sketches. "Poor dear, his drawing is even worse than his spelling. Well, we shall just keep our eyes open, Todd. That is all we can do."

Ducks and geese and other birds landed on the lake or beside it as they ambled along the bank. Were they what Cousin Albert had tried to draw, the "grand convocation" of the world's species?

That would agree with what the lady in the Natural History Museum had guessed — that the sketches were bird skeletons. But why had he drawn birds? And why just their skeletons?

He pushed the puzzle to the back of his mind and listened to his aunt. "You know, London is unique," she was saying. "No place on earth simply *throbs with history* as it does here." One navy-suited arm swept passionately off to the east, the other to the west.

A small dog barked — the same terrier they had seen at Speaker's Corner. Aunt Morbelia turned her eyes on the terrier, which instantly sat down and closed its mouth.

"However," she continued, "I promise not to lecture. Of course, I am delighted to answer questions."

"Good," said Jeff. "Does anybody here ever go to a movie or anything American like that?"

"Certainly, but I would prefer to attend plays. London has the best theater in the world."

"Funny plays?" Todd asked hopefully.

"Yes, of course, and one serious play — one that shows people dealing with a major event — something that causes them to consider their lives and change direction. We have an example of that right in our family — Cousin Albert."

"Changed by what he learned about his dad, you mean?" said Todd.

"Indeed. Before that, I think he was unaware of many things. He was so gentle and idealistic, himself, that he was unable to understand his own father's character.

"His mother told him the truth, of course, after his father's death. Then he had a dream which affected him permanently, I believe. He wrote me all about it."

"But *he* hadn't done anything wrong," said Todd.

"True, but in my cousin's dream he was present at his father's trial by the animals. He listened to their testimony and heard the verdict of death, which they carried out as I described in the gamekeeper's cottage."

She broke off, her attention on the lake. "Do you see the lovely black swans over there? Such elegant birds, although their feathers lack the sheen of a raven's, as you shall see at the Tower of London. I always enjoy watching the Tower ravens strutting about."

Todd and Jeff looked at each other in frustration. "Cousin Albert saw his father being tried by animals *in a dream?*" asked Jeff.

"Oh, yes. He wrote about how vivid it was. Unfortunately, it left him still wondering what had happened to his friend, the gamekeeper.

"Anyway, after his dream, Cousin Albert spent most of his life in the forest. I was told he could imitate bird sounds to perfection, for anyone who would listen."

"Hrr, hrrr," snarled the wiry terrier, straining at his leash. Teeth bared, he came at Aunt Morbelia from behind a nearby clump of shrubbery, dragging his owner with him.

"Naughty Winston! Naughty, naughty!" whimpered the lady in the pink jogging suit. With a heroic tug, she hauled him in and scooped him up. She gave them all an odd, indecipherable look and wandered back toward the shrubbery.

Aunt Morbelia shook her head. "Why some people choose to own animals is simply beyond my comprehension."

"So go on," urged Todd.

"Oh yes. Well, the people heard poor Cousin Albert chirping all over the marketplace — so to speak —

claiming that he was talking to the birds, and they decided he belonged in the insane asylum. His wife pleaded for him — even hired a lawyer, I believe — but it was hopeless.

"He was incarcerated around 1955, when he was in his late thirties. For someone who loved the outdoors as he did, the asylum must have been a cruel prison. I wrote to the doctors there, but they never replied, and eventually I gave up." Her voice was low now, and sad.

"Poor, dear Albert. He died in a few years, and that is how Harrowwood passed to me and my sisters as the next of kin. We thought that he simply willed himself to die."

"What a bummer!" said Todd. "He didn't hurt anybody. He was just different."

Jeff said, "Yeah, people are like that, though. You know that little dweeb in eighth grade? Billy Humphrey? Well, it's the same thing, kind of."

Todd nodded, thinking he would be nicer to Billy the next time he saw him.

Jeff elbowed him in the ribs. "Race you to that statue."

Todd ran as fast as he could, knowing that if he really poured it on he could beat Jeff. Jeff was a fast tackle, but a tackle, after all, not an end. Ends were always faster. When he got to the statue he turned and leaned against it, hands casually stuck in his pockets.

"You didn't win . . . by much," Jeff said, his sides heaving. They rested against the statue of Achilles and panted companionably.

"Hey, look back there, where Aunt M is," said Jeff when he quit puffing. "It's that lady and her dog again."

"Yup," Todd said. "They've been with us ever since we got here."

Jeff's normally sunny face clouded over. "Oh, come on. Like yesterday, you mean?"

"Well, there she is." Todd squinted at the pink figure that was right behind his aunt. If she had on very high heels and a black dress and a funny hat . . . Nah, no way. The girl in the spiky heels was thinner and much younger.

"Todd? So, what's going on?"

"You got me. But let's go all over this park. It's huge on the map. It even runs into another park. And if that lady and her dog follow us, well, then we'll know something."

"Okay, Sherlock." Jeff was silent briefly. Then he said, "Todd, are all your vacations like this?"

"Didn't you know? This is my first vacation!"

8

Who's That in the Orange Hair?

Todd buried his toast in marmalade and thought about the day before, in Hyde Park. Except for a bunch of birds, they hadn't seen a single thing he could link to Cousin Albert's journal. They had read every word on every statue and plaque, too.

"When's Aunt M coming back?" Jeff asked, lifting the tiny red plaid cosy off of his boiled egg. "Have you told her what we talked about last night?"

"Not yet, no. She'll be back from the solicitor's any minute, though. She said going to the Tower of London was a great idea, especially since Cousin Albert spent a lot of time there. Did I show you this part?" He pulled the journal out of his pocket.

"Here, this made me feel pretty good. He's a whole lot worse speller than I am." Todd held the book open for Jeff to read.

Tower of London, 22 May 1951.

Been hear so often they gave me a pass.
New yesterday — aãaüuuü. Progruss slow
but steady. They are a closed and closed-
mowth sociuty. Very rituullistic as well.

Jeff shook his head. "Did you show this to Aunt M?"

"Yeah, and she doesn't get it either. But I still have to ask her about the mariner and albatross part. Maybe she'll know about that."

Mrs. Dwiddle bustled in from the kitchen. "How are you doing, luv?" She patted Todd's shoulder. "Such a treat it is, you here from America, and looking just like all the Fearings."

She put her other hand on Jeff's shoulder and patted him, too. "I miss my own two boys, now they're grown. There's nothing like having boys around to stir things up."

"Mom says all I have to do is walk into a room and something breaks," said Jeff. "We can break something for you if it'll make you feel better."

They were laughing when Aunt Morbelia joined them and poured herself a cup of tea. Mrs. Dwiddle left to make up the beds, and Aunt Morbelia reviewed her meeting with the solicitor. "I do not see how we can keep the estate, Todd. It is so huge that it absolutely eats money." She added milk and sugar to her tea and stirred halfheartedly.

"Could you sell the house and keep the forest?"

"No one wants one of those old stone monstrosities, Todd. They like the wooded lands, just as we do." She sounded old and defeated, not a bit like herself.

"Well, you don't have to sell it today," he said. "Maybe Dad'll have an idea. We'll call him. But first, do you want to hear something weird?"

Knowing she'd say yes, he rushed on. "See, Jeff and I were talking last night and — well — you remember that girl at the Natural History Museum, right? And I really wasn't interested in her. *No way!* Well, yesterday in the park, that lady in the pink warm-up suit was right behind us every time we turned around. So that's two times in two days!"

Aunt Morbelia leaned back against her chair and sipped her tea. "Are you referring to that short, round, middle-aged woman in exercise clothes, with the ill-behaved dog?"

"Yeah! That's the one!"

"What about her?"

"She followed us! All the way from Speaker's Corner to the Albert Memorial! She never even looked at the stuff in the park. She just looked at us! For hours!"

"Of course I remember her, but consider what you

are saying, Todd. You are suggesting that the most normal-looking British homemaker I have ever seen put on a vivid pink outfit and took her yapping dog into Hyde Park in order to follow three ordinary American tourists."

"Geez, Aunt M, don't think of it like that!" said Jeff, now pacing the dining room. "What if the lady and the girl are sort of . . . well . . . amateurs? Maybe they're reporting to somebody."

Aunt Morbelia looked from Jeff to Todd as if both of them had left their brains in America. Quietly she said, "Oh, bushwah. I know I am preoccupied with Harrowwood's problems — and distracted by changes since I was last here — but I still know what is going on around me. I can think of no reason why anyone should even care that we are here, let alone follow our every move.

"Please, boys, put these thoughts out of your mind. We are supposed to be on holiday! Now then, I am ready for the Tower of London. How about you?"

Pretty logical, Todd thought. So why do I still feel like a sitting duck? He glanced at Jeff, who was nodding politely, but not with the look of someone who had been convinced.

Like his friend, Todd yielded for now. "Okay, but we just *could* be right, you know. I'll go get my camera."

Thanks to the Underground, they were walking

toward the Tower within minutes. "London is more fun than anything at home," Todd said as they approached the ticket line.

"London is more fun than anywhere in the world," replied Aunt Morbelia. "The number of tourists here is staggering."

"And they're all in line ahead of us," said Jeff.

"Just enjoy being here then," she said.

As they inched forward, Todd remembered his question about the journal. "See here?" he asked his aunt, handing her the journal. "Here where he says he's an 'Ancient Marriner' with an albatross around his neck. What does he mean by that?"

"Hmm, yes, I remember this part. Let me think now." She closed her eyes briefly, then opened them and began reciting.

> *For all averred, I had killed the bird*
> *That made the breeze to blow,*
> *Ah wretch! said they, the bird to slay,*
> *That made the breeze to blow!*

She stopped and waited for their reaction.

"That's great," Todd said.

"Yes. *The Rime of The Ancient Mariner.* It is the story of an old seaman who killed an albatross. His mates thought his killing of the bird had stopped the winds, stranding them in the middle of the ocean, so they hung it round his neck as a punishment."

Todd frowned. "Do you think Cousin Albert thought of his dad as *his* albatross?"

"His burden of guilt, yes — although he had no reason to feel responsible for his father's crimes." She appeared to shake her shoulders and stand taller. "But we are here at the Tower now — a fascinating place, my favorite in all of London."

Todd considered the enormous stone fortress on their left. What would it have been like to live inside those gray walls? Cold, he thought, remembering Harrowwood House.

"I can hear the wheels going round," said his aunt.

"I was thinking about living there."

"Mainly they died," Jeff said. "Nobody lived very long in the old days, remember?"

And finally, they were inside the Tower grounds, where Aunt Morbelia said, "We must take a tour here. The guides are former servicemen and they are world famous."

"Hey, the Major's brother Farley was a serviceman and he *loves* to talk. This's something he could do," said Todd.

"Welcome to the Tower of London!" boomed a bulky man, resplendent in a red-and-gold Beefeater's uniform. He began lecturing, starting with the first days of the Tower, built by William the Conqueror to impress his new English subjects.

After only a few minutes Todd whispered to Jeff, "If history was like this at home, it'd be okay."

"And having been brought in through Traitor's Gate," the guide said, "young Princess Elizabeth sat down — on these very stones — and defied the Tower guards.

"Now none of us can imagine the courage that took. Remember, Bloody Mary, her half-sister, was on the throne then, and she was busily hanging or beheading people every week. She truly wanted her younger sister — this very clever, non-Catholic Elizabeth — *out of her way.*"

"Geez, why?" Todd whispered to his aunt.

"Famous case of sibling rivalry," she whispered back. "Mary thought Elizabeth wanted her crown. Mary was always insecure — not a bit like Elizabeth."

Concluding his story of Elizabeth I, "who reigned for forty-four glorious years," the guide led them farther into the grounds, which had grown to include thirteen linked towers. While he lectured, Todd looked around at their group, which appeared to have come mainly from the United States or the Orient.

One very noticeable teenage girl wore a tight black jumpsuit and had orange hair poking upright in spikes. It was neon pink down near the scalp.

"Punk rock look," Todd said, pointing her out to his aunt.

"Colorful, isn't it?" she replied. "And she has magnificent eyes. Come along. We are going to the Bloody Tower. Here is where the guide says that the little princes were murdered by their uncle, Richard III, but don't you believe it."

As the morning went on, Todd heard one horrific story after another, many revolving around the execution block. Most of the victims had gone meekly to their beheadings, but not the Countess of Salisbury. She had screamed and tried repeatedly to run away from her executioners.

"I do so admire the Countess," whispered Todd's aunt. "But now you can see why the Red Queen is always hollering 'Off with their heads' in *Alice in Wonderland*. Beheading was the royal answer to problems for years."

At the end of the tour, Todd and Jeff agreed that the Tower was a fine place, and yet they had no idea why Cousin Albert had come here so often. "How is all this connected to the Natural History Museum and Hyde Park?" Todd wondered aloud as they strolled across the grass of Tower Green.

Neither his aunt nor Jeff could suggest an answer. "What would you two like to do now?" she asked. "I want to walk about the Green for a bit and watch the ravens. Such fascinating birds, though nearly always creatures of ill omen. They mate for life, did you know that?"

"Nope, but they're sure big," Jeff observed. "Bigger than crows even."

"Yes. Remember Edgar Allan Poe's raven, always croaking 'Nevermore' in the poem?" She smiled. "Here they say that the Tower will fall if ever the ravens leave."

Ravens, Todd thought. *More ravens.* "Why don't they just take off sometime?"

"They cannot. Their wings have been clipped." She gave him a thoughtful look. "It would be more of a test of the legend if the ravens were given a fair chance, don't you think? Go along now. I shall wait here."

Todd and Jeff decided to check out the White Tower, with its dungeons and medieval armor. As they mounted the Tower steps, Todd said, "They've got ravens on the brain here. And remember Albert Leatherhead's dream? That was a raven, too. And Cousin Albert's drawings are birds, and there were tons of birds all over Hyde Park. It's weird, but maybe we're getting somewhere after all."

They were in the armouries, staring in awe at Henry VIII, massive and sinister-looking in his gold-plated armor, when Jeff hissed, "Guess what? That weirdo with the orange hair is right behind us."

Todd stared at Henry VIII and wondered how anyone ever went to the bathroom wearing all that metal. He refused to think that someone was following them again.

"Did you hear me?" Jeff said in Todd's ear.

"Yeah, but other people from our group are in here."

"Uh-huh, but this is the only one who was right behind us when we were down in the dungeons, *and* on the second floor, and now *here*."

Todd's shoulders slumped. He had been so caught up in what they were doing that he hadn't noticed anything else — just like Aunt Morbelia had been all weekend, he realized.

"Let's test her the way we tested the dog lady yesterday," Jeff suggested.

"Got it," said Todd, turning swiftly for the exit. He led them as they zipped in and out of areas at random, then ran downstairs to St. John's Chapel, which Aunt Morbelia had said they must see. Here they pretended to admire the arches and sturdy columns and geometric designs of William the Conqueror's small Norman chapel.

Todd soon found he was not pretending. This place felt real. He could imagine being a kid here on a winter morning, trying to pay attention to the service so he wouldn't get in trouble, rubbing his arms to keep warm. Wishing for a fire instead of a sermon. Wishing for clothes lined with fur. Thick, furry boots and a big, fur-lined cloak —

"Ssst. Look over your left shoulder," Jeff muttered.

Todd forced himself back to the real world. He swiveled his head just enough to the left, and there she was, with that dumb glow-orange hair. How did people get their hair to stick up like that, anyhow?

Abruptly he said, "Let's get Aunt Morbelia and go for lunch."

They chose the restaurant on the grounds, and Orange-Hair went along, though very discreetly. She didn't sit in the same room, but they knew she was in the next one, right around the corner. Todd's Toad-in-the-Hole, a sausage in a cold pastry casing, settled unhappily in his stomach.

After lunch the girl just happened to be at the Bloody Tower when they revisited it so Aunt Morbelia could explain why Richard III, beloved uncle of the little princes, would never have considered murdering his nephews.

Moreover, when they got onto the train going home, Todd was sure she'd gotten on as well, only two cars down. I just don't get it, he thought. That sentence played over and over in his mind, like an electronic device stuck in one position. Maybe Aunt Morbelia could shrug off the business at the Natural History

Museum or in Hyde Park, but now that they had been followed for the third day in a row, he could not.

He couldn't concentrate on crazy Cousin Albert's journal or anything else until he had resolved this problem. What possible reason could anyone have for following them around London? By now, though, he felt he knew who Orange-Hair was. Turning to Jeff, he asked, "She remind you of anybody?"

"Yup. Same girl, different clothes."

In the seat ahead of them, Aunt Morbelia was going over notes she'd made at the meeting with her solicitor. She has no idea, Todd thought. She's got other stuff on her mind.

But he and Jeff knew for sure now. They really were being followed. They were being watched. Shadowed. Spied upon. Stalked.

Todd's skin prickled all over and he shivered.

9

The Man in the Pub

"Every visitor to London comes here, and we all feed these pigeons. They must be the happiest birds in England," said Aunt Morbelia, on their arrival at Trafalgar Square.

Todd took a picture of Jeff, head to head with one of the huge stone lions in the square, and then Jeff took Todd's. From her handbag, Aunt Morbelia produced a napkin-wrapped packet. "For the pigeons," she said, settling herself on the concrete base of one of the lions.

Jeff and Todd divided the leftover breakfast toast and tossed small bits up into the air. Todd began inching toward a small, crippled pigeon balancing on one claw at the edge of the flock.

Jeff called softly to Todd from the other side of the flock. "Come over here."

When he got there, Jeff whispered, "Over there —

behind that lion." He nodded in the direction of the National Gallery, which was behind the girl, who was behind the lion.

"You mean Orange-Hair?"

"Spot on, mate." Jeff made a face.

They stayed at Trafalgar Square a while longer, feeding the little lame pigeon and wondering what Orange-Hair was up to. All they could think of to do was to keep track of her. She was much sneakier than the woman in the hot-pink warmup suit, but on the way home Todd thought they had eluded her at last, in the Underground station.

However, only a few minutes after they'd gone inside, he saw her stride smartly past the front door of Ye Olde Saxon. Hair in those defiant, orange spikes, eyes forward, she marched up the street toward Gloucester Road.

Now she knows where we're staying, he thought, heading for their room to tell Jeff.

After they came in from dinner that evening, Aunt Morbelia wanted them to sit and visit with the Dwiddles. Fortunately, the Major said, "Top of Gloucester Road, boys, then right on Cromwell. Only two blocks to The Squinting Cat. They have darts there."

Major Dwiddle beamed with the forgivable pride of a good host. "Morbelia just happened to mention you like darts, and this is a family place — quiet-like and friendly."

"Be back by ten," added Todd's aunt. "It will be getting dark then and I shall proceed to get very nervous if you are not here."

Mm-hmm, Todd thought, especially if you knew we were being followed. If I told you that Orange-Hair followed us home, there'd be no darts game.

But he wanted a night out in London with Jeff — just the two of them, on their own. Surely, he told himself, no one will follow us *tonight*. Why would anyone care if we go out for a game of darts? He pushed the idea into the farthest corner of his mind.

"Well, guess we'll go then," he said, eager to be off.

"Dear me, I almost forgot," said Emma Dwiddle, reaching into her knitting basket. "This came in the noon post. I put it in your mail pigeonhole, but you must not have looked." She handed Todd a small, tan envelope.

He read the return address: *Natural History Museum.* "Now we're getting somewhere." Hope rose within him as he took a sheet of paper from the envelope. Hope descended as he read the curator's message:

Although many on our staff looked at the pictures from your relative's diary, I regret that we can offer you no specific information. Our best guess is that the artist was trying to depict large birds of the corvid family —

crows and ravens, probably — with special attention to
the heads of the birds, as you may have noted.

Respectfully,

Fiona Witherspoon,

Assoc. Curator, Ornithology

He passed the letter to his aunt, who read it
quickly and then said, "Well, Todd, we knew that
Cousin Albert was not an artist and he disliked writing,
which explains why the journal entries are so brief. He
was brilliant — I know that — and I am coming to believe he was dyslexic, and enormously frustrated by the
problem."

She shrugged. "Of course, you understand all that,
but back then we knew very little about learning differ-
ences." She patted his shoulder and he knew she was
trying to find a way to cheer him up.

"It's okay," he said, rereading the letter, his eyes
drawn to the word *ravens*. Here they were again. Also,
the curator had caught something he had missed.
Cousin Albert had drawn more heads of birds than
whole birds . . . probably for a reason.

The museum staff made no mention of the strange
symbols at the back of the journal, yet Todd felt sure
they were significant. Certainly they had been important to poor, crazy Cousin Albert.

"So . . . can we leave now?" prompted Jeff.

"Sure."

Outside, heading up the street, Jeff kept looking back over his shoulder.

"I don't see her," said Todd. "But, just in case, how about a little road work?"

Jeff grinned. "Brilliant. Let's boogie!"

They raced up the street and wheeled right at Cromwell Road. Two short blocks later they dashed into The Squinting Cat, where they collapsed, laughing, into a wooden booth. This time only a track star could have followed them.

"Cool place," Todd said, appreciating the mellow sheen of the dark paneling. Pictures of royalty hung everywhere, as if they were family, and especially photos of the young princes, William and Harry.

In one corner, two women visited over a meal. In a booth on the left wall, a young man smiled at his girl as they ate dinner. And behind the bar sat a man watching television. The major's description of a "quiet" place was deadly accurate.

"Let's get some Cokes and the darts," Jeff said.

Todd gave their order and they watched TV while they waited. An alert, black-and-white collie-type dog was herding a few sheep down an emerald green slope. From afar, a man in a mackintosh sent urgent whistles to the dog.

"Name's Jocky," said the bartender, pointing to the

dog. " 'E'll win it again this year like 'e did last, you wite and see. That chap talks to 'is dog with those whistles, 'e does."

Todd and Jeff nodded.

The bartender gave them a sharp look. "You the Americans stayin' with Major Dwiddle?"

"Yessir," Todd said, watching the screen. Jocky looked like a terrific dog. "What kind of contest is that?"

At his question, a delighted smile spread across the bartender's face. He pushed their Cokes toward them, got comfortable on his stool, and began a detailed explanation of the Scottish sheepdog trials. Todd and Jeff tried to be polite, and not look wistfully over at the dartboard.

Just as Todd was ready to kick the bar in frustration, the man stopped talking. Before he could say any more, Todd jumped off his stool. "Hey, thanks a lot. Guess we'll play darts now."

He and Jeff each took a set of darts and began warming up. "This is going to take a lot of Coke," Jeff said, squinting at the Triple 20. "Maybe some potato chips, too."

When it was his turn, Todd sent his third dart into the center of the bull's-eye. "Hey, look at that! Why can't I do that during a real game?"

"Great shot," Jeff said as he got ready on the

throwing line. "We've got an audience, too. You see that guy in the corner? He keeps looking over here."

"I didn't even know he was there. We must look pretty bad, hunh?"

Jeff threw his first dart. "Heck, we're kids. What does he expect? But he can quit staring any time. I hate that when I'm trying to concentrate."

Me, too, thought Todd. But what if he's interested in us, not the darts? Oh, poop, there I go again.

As he waited for his turn, Todd glanced at the corner off and on — just the idle glances of someone who was bored, he told himself. The man was sitting all hunched over, as if absorbed in the contents of the beer mug in front of him.

Todd stored a mental picture. A mop of messy brown hair spilled down into the man's eyes, and he wore extremely baggy clothes — some black, some a dark green plaid. His face was dirty, but he had on a pair of good leather boots, at odds with the rest of him.

"Hey, hey!" Jeff exulted. "A Triple Twenty! Look at that!"

"Good thing we haven't started a game."

"We haven't?" Jeff tried to look innocent.

"No way! Nobody said, *Okay let's have a game*, or anything like that! We were *just practicing*."

"You wouldn't say that if it'd been *your* Triple Twenty!"

"Look, I got an eyeball, and we didn't count that!"

Jeff relaxed and began to grin. "Oh, boy. Another hall-of-famer. You got an *eyeball*. Oh, geez."

Eyeball, thought Todd. It's wrong somehow. He tried to picture the word, experimenting with a few letters. He wrote with his finger on their table. Oh yeah, he had it now. "I mean *bull's-eye*. You know what I mean!"

"I know, I know, but this's a really good one. A classic! Almost as good as *hacky-turctor*."

If you say so, Todd thought, smiling now. Jeff had insisted, years ago, that neither one of them should ever say *helicopter* as long as they lived.

"Okay, so *now* we're starting a game," Jeff announced. "This'll probably be more like it. We're getting better."

"You go," Todd said. He pretended to watch Jeff's scores while sneaking peeks at the guy in the corner, who hardly ever took his eyes off them.

But why? Was the guy far away from his own kids and lonesome, maybe? Perhaps he hadn't ever heard Americans talk before, except on TV. Surely he couldn't be here just to watch them.

Todd felt his stomach go into a cramp. Could yet another person . . . ?

"I'm down to three eighty-five in only two turns,"

Jeff said, sitting down. "Yup, we can get good at this." He leaned over and whispered, "What's with him? He's still staring."

Todd whispered back. "I hate to say it, but I think we're his job for the evening."

Todd threw his next three darts fast. He couldn't watch the man and throw darts at the same time, and he thought he should be watching the man. The result was embarrassing.

"Twenty-four lousy points for a whole turn," he said, flopping down on the bench beside Jeff.

"Yeah, but who can concentrate? If I was a grown-up I'd go over there and ask that creep what he thinks he's doing." Jeff made his hands into fists.

"Well, he hasn't really done anything. Go on, it's your turn. Let's try to forget him."

"I guess we can try. So what're we going to do about the journal? What's our next step?" Jeff sent a dart neatly into the Double Ten space — a real coup, as double-number spaces were tiny.

"We have to think," Todd said, pulling the journal out of his pocket. Poor crazy Cousin Albert and his little drawings. Bird heads, he thought, remembering the curator's note. And Aunt Morbelia had said he could imitate bird sounds perfectly.

Bird sounds? he thought suddenly.

"Sure! Bird sounds!" he yelped.

Jeff looked startled. "Not so loud. He's really giving us the eye."

"But did you hear me?"

"The whole place can hear you!"

"Okay, okay," Todd said, lowering his voice. "But I'll bet I'm right. I'll bet he was trying to write the sounds birds made!"

"Yup, makes sense. Hey, Todd, why don't you give that guy one of your Aunt Morbelia looks? Let him know we know he's bugging us."

But when Todd made a point of staring at him, the man merely lowered his eyes and gazed down into his mug.

That's the same beer he started with, Todd realized. He just takes little sips now and then. He's not here to drink, that's for sure. And now he knows *we know* what he's doing, and I don't think he gives a bean. No skin off his nose.

Jeff and Todd stood shoulder to shoulder on the throwing line, sleeking back the feathers on their darts, apparently eying the target in front of them. "We have to *do something*," Jeff whispered. "If we try to leave, I bet he'll follow us."

"I've got an idea. Meet me in the men's room in one minute." Todd sauntered over to their bench and put his darts down.

"Be right back," he said loudly, wanting the man in the corner to hear.

Todd had been in the men's room only a few seconds when Jeff burst through the door. "We have to do something *quick!* I think he's following me!"

10

No Safe Place

"I'm back here!" cried Todd. "Hurry up!"

Jeff ran to the back corner of the men's room, where Todd was waiting by an open window. "You go first," Jeff said. "Jump up there. Yeah, yeah. Now grab my hands and let yourself down."

In seconds, Todd was in the alley behind The Squinting Cat. Jeff tumbled out after him, righted himself with Todd's help, and they were off and running — not like thundering buffalo, but swift and silent like cats. They could hear Coach Jensen calling the drill. *Fast feet, cat feet!* They gave it all they had, as if Coach were demanding more speed, flying down the scary dark alley toward the light, where alley met sidewalk.

They hit the sidewalk on Cromwell Road, angled sharp left, and never even slowed down. Racing the blocks to Gloucester Road, they made another left and kept on going, starting to breathe hard now, all the way to Ye Olde Saxon.

"Mercy!" cried Mrs. Dwiddle as they exploded through her front door and into the parlor.

They leaned against the sofa and concentrated on breathing. Too bad Coach wasn't here to see what they could do when they had to. "Sorry," Todd gasped. "Where's my aunt?"

"In the tub, dear. And Major Dwiddle has retired for the night. Do you need help? Are you all right?"

Todd stood up straight. "We're fine . . . just out of breath . . . from racing. We'll go . . . see my aunt."

A brief chat through the bathroom door reassured Aunt Morbelia that they were home, and the boys went on to their room. Todd closed the door behind them and said, "Okay, this is too much. I don't know why we're being followed, but I'm sick of it! And if we try to tell Aunt Morbelia about tonight, it'll sound dumb because we haven't got any proof!"

"Well, we'd better get some." Jeff kicked first one shoe then the other across the room.

After a short silence Todd said, "I've got an idea."

The next day was Tuesday, their sixth day in England. They lingered over breakfast, visiting with Farley Dwiddle, who'd dropped in unexpectedly, and then they had to rush to catch the bus to Stonehenge. They practically ran up the street to the tourist agency through which Aunt Morbelia had been making all of their arrangements.

"Ah, Stonehenge — the Giants' Dance — my favorite place in England," Aunt Morbelia had said the night before, when Todd suggested they go there. He refrained from telling her she said that about every place they went.

Now, as they passed the meat market, she said, "Remind me to run in there and get two chickens for Emma on our way home."

"People really buy them like that, feathers and all?" asked Jeff. "I hate thinking about what my meat looked like when it was alive. It all looks like somebody's pet." He frowned at the row of rabbits and poultry, dangling by their feet in the window.

Todd's aunt chuckled. "Yes, and *I* wish it were all in a freezer. An Englishman had that idea first, you know."

"You mean the Father of the Freezer?" joked Todd.

"Exactly. Francis Bacon. A famous writer. He died of a fatal bronchitis he got whilst proving you could preserve meat by keeping it cold. He stuffed chickens with snow, I believe."

At the tourist agency, they boarded the waiting coach. Aunt Morbelia settled partway down the aisle on the right, and the boys sat behind her.

Todd waited until they were out of city traffic and

rolling smoothly southwest. Then he dropped his ball-point pen, giving it a good push so that it tumbled down the long aisle. "Oh, darnit," he said loudly, getting up. He managed to stumble his way down the aisle.

"Oops. Sorry," he told a young woman, clutching the back of her seat as he apologized.

"Sorry about that," he said to a pair of middle-aged women as he grabbed hold of their armrest.

A few stumbles later he had retrieved the pen and had worked his way back to his own seat, where Jeff was hiding under his jacket, laughing. When Todd sat down, he stuck his head out and said, "Well?"

"I don't think so, and I got a pretty good look at everybody. There are still four rows ahead of us, though."

"They're mine," Jeff said, stepping over Todd. He moseyed up the aisle to the blue-uniformed driver, an unremarkable man except for his head of thick, dark red hair.

Todd watched as Jeff talked to the driver and then started back down the aisle. "Nice hat," Jeff said to someone in the first row. And then he was pushing past Todd to his place by the window.

At the look on Jeff's face, Todd said, "Who?"

"I'm not sure — just guessing."

"Where?"

"Right behind the driver. You go check, okay?"

Todd made his way up the aisle — past row four, row three, row two. Then he lurched forward and to the left. "Oops. Brand new feet. Can't do a thing with them, ha ha."

He clutched the pole between row one and the front steps. As he regained his footing, he gave the people behind the driver a careful look. Two women. One young, one middle-aged. They must have left the terrier at home.

To the driver he said, "How long till we get there?"

"Maybe half an hour. Your mate asked the same thing. Don't you talk to one another?" He gave Todd a frigid look from a pair of the bluest eyes on earth. They were so blue they didn't even look real, yet the power of that stare was unmistakable.

"Uh . . . he . . . uh . . . he said he didn't hear what you said, so I . . . came up here. Bye." Todd hurried back to the security of his seat.

"Yeah, yeah?" Jeff shook his arm.

"The driver, too. Our hire car driver."

Jeff's eyes grew big. "No way!"

"Yup. I think he's wearing a wig and contact lenses. Take a look at him when we get off."

"Three of them. *Here.* Wow." Jeff sat very still.

For a while neither of them said anything. Todd thought harder than he ever had before, much harder than when he'd taken the special math test to qualify for algebra in the fall. He needed to make sense of what was happening to them here . . . and why. There was an answer, and he had to find it.

"Jeff," he whispered, "they're *trying* to scare us."

"Yeah, and it's working."

"What if . . ." Todd stopped. His idea seemed awfully far-fetched. But then he made himself go on. "What if all of this is connected somehow? I mean, people maybe using the gamekeeper's cottage . . . and the noises we heard at Harrowwood . . . and our being followed everywhere? All of it."

Jeff fished in his pocket for a stick of gum, unwrapped it, stuck it in his mouth, and ruminated in absolute silence. Todd knew enough to wait, and in time Jeff nodded and said, "Probably. You think this guy was the guy in the pub last night?"

Todd nodded solemnly.

"Something else," Jeff went on. "It sure is creepy how they always know where we're going."

Again they slipped into a thoughtful silence, relieved when at last the coach slowed down and turned into the car park across the road from Stonehenge.

"I'll stick with Aunt Morbelia," Todd whispered.

"I know." Jeff stood up very straight, and for a second Todd was reminded of Jeff's dad, a big, solid man. A dependable rock.

As they left the bus, Todd kept his eyes on the two

women. Today, the young one was wearing big hair —
mouse brown in color — and a yucky beige dress that
hung unevenly just above a pair of brown sandals.

The older woman had traded her pink warmup suit
for a tentlike flowered dress in orange and yellow. Her
hair was mousy, too, but it looked like her own.
Perched on top of it was a masculine-looking white golf
cap with a broad green bill that shaded her eyes. Oh
yeah, *nice hat,* Todd thought, grinning as he recalled
Jeff's earlier comment.

"You will remember Stonehenge all your life,"
Aunt Morbelia said as they went toward the ticket
booth. "When I came here as a young woman, we could
walk among the stones and touch them, which you cannot now. I always wondered what rituals went on in that
giant circle, wishing the stones could talk.

"One time I was standing on the largest of the
bluestones, the Altar Stone, and I had a revelation. It
had been a gray, rainy day, and my sisters and I were
here together, revisiting sights that meant something to
us as a family. Our parents had been dead only a month
or so.

"I was depressed, you see, and standing there on
the Altar Stone, when suddenly the sun came out and
shone down, just on me. Just on that one place. Only
for a few minutes.

"But after that I was heartened somehow. On the

way home, I told my sisters we should sell the house in Yorkshire and move to America. Start a new life. And Cordelia and Ophelia agreed straightaway. They said I was a clever girl to think of it, and what had taken me so long." She shook her head and laughed softly, pleasured by the memory.

At the entrance, Todd and Jeff dawdled on purpose, buying postcards to send home. Jeff went to the men's room while Todd bought cold drinks for them and hot tea for his aunt. He watched the two women, and when they started into the tunnel under the road — the walkway to Stonehenge — he and Jeff and Aunt Morbelia were right behind them.

"Where's the driver?" Jeff whispered in the dimness of the tunnel.

"With the bus. I'll do him when we go back," Todd said, slipping the lens cap off his camera. He held it in what he prayed would be a good position, and as soon as the two women stepped into the light, he snapped a picture. Now he had a back view at least.

"Crikey!" cried the girl, whirling around.

Todd swiveled his camera off to the right. Snap! Snap! Two quick pictures. "Got their campsite on film," he announced. "They'll like that." He got a nasty look from the young woman and a strange one from his aunt.

"Friends of Jeff's brother, Duane," he said, lying fluently. "They camped out here last year."

"I see," said Aunt Morbelia. She opened her guide-book to read them her favorite Stonehenge facts. Jeff winked at Todd and bent down to pluck a wildflower.

"Oh! Oooh! Yow! Geez, that hurts!" Hugging his thumb to his chest, Jeff carried on as everyone watched.

Snap! Snap! Side views this time, and Todd was fairly sure the women were unaware of what he was doing.

"Stupid bee!" Jeff hollered. "Musta been a bum-blebee!" He began sucking his thumb, all the time stamping one foot.

Snap! Snap! Even better profiles, but Todd thought the older woman had figured out what was happening.

"Jeff," said Aunt Morbelia, "put mud on the place where you were stung."

"Mmm," Jeff mumbled around his thumb, "iss geh-ing beh-er mow."

They stayed at Stonehenge for some time, listen-ing to Aunt Morbelia as they circled the prehistoric site. Todd took several more pictures, but the two women were now being careful to stay behind him and his camera.

"A remarkable engineering feat," Aunt Morbelia said, referring to the moving and lifting of the enor-mous stones. "And they found cremated bodies in a se-ries of holes around the perimeter. I wonder whether it was an honor to be buried like that, or if those people were sacrifices to an ancient god?"

By this time Jeff had stopped sucking his thumb. He looked absolutely normal until all of a sudden he crashed to the pavement. "Oh, oh, my ankle, my ankle!" he moaned, his face contorted as he bent over.

Snap! Snap! Front views this time. That ought to do it, Todd thought happily as he put the lens cap back on his camera. The girl had disguised herself pretty well, with all that big hair and tons of makeup, but she should have worn the glasses to hide her eyes, a most distinctive feature. He knew his aunt would recognize her.

"Do not move, Jeff," Aunt Morbelia was saying. "Just let me feel the ankle."

Jeff whimpered and closed his eyes while she examined his right ankle.

Wearing his most concerned face, Todd looked on. Jeff was really good at this.

"Let me try a little weight on it," Jeff said. "It's feeling better."

Todd and Aunt Morbelia helped him up. Jeff leaned on their arms and limped convincingly toward the tunnel and the car park.

Went great, Todd thought, still glowing with self-congratulation. He thought Aunt Morbelia would recognize the woman, too. She hadn't bothered to disguise herself much. It was easy to imagine her in the hot-pink warmup suit, minus the dopey hat, and with her hair piled on top of her head as it had been on Sunday in Hyde Park.

As they neared the coach, he took a picture of the driver, who was standing by the open door, his face in profile. He didn't even see me do it, Todd thought as he stowed his camera in its case.

For the remainder of the day, from a restaurant in Salisbury to the town's famous cathedral, Todd watched the two women grow bolder and bolder. They stayed behind his group, but dismayingly close. Once, he was sure the older woman was looking down into Aunt Morbelia's handbag.

The girl cracked her gum continuously and now and then darted poisonous glances at him that Todd knew he was meant to see. Never, not for even a minute, could he and Jeff forget they were being followed.

"Meanest-looking girl I ever saw," Todd observed as they left the cathedral.

"Aunt M caught her staring once and gave her a good one back." Jeff grinned. "It was kind of a tie, I thought."

On the way home, Todd's aunt read a book. She didn't notice that the driver of the coach kept glancing back at them, all the way to London. As they entered the outskirts of the city, Jeff squirmed in his seat. "Man, we just can't get away from these people."

"Well, we're *going to!*" said Todd. "Remember, soon as we get back, we look for a quickie-photo shop."

They spent the last minutes of the trip trying to figure out how their stalkers always knew where they were going — a significant question, Todd thought. He dropped off his roll of film at a shop on Cromwell Road, and they bought two chickens for Mrs. Dwiddle. Not until they were walking in the door at Ye Olde Saxon did Todd realize he hadn't thought of Cousin Albert's journal all day.

11

The Birds' Message

They had dinner with the Dwiddles Tuesday night. As a treat for Aunt Morbelia and the Major's brother, who had invited himself to dinner, Emma Dwiddle had fixed steak-and-kidney pie, an old British favorite.

"Kidneys, *gross*," Jeff said when they were in their room later. "I never eat *guts*."

"Here," Todd said, handing him a chocolate candy bar from the supply in his suitcase. British candy and desserts were outstanding. Here, it seemed, was an entire country that understood the importance of sweets.

Todd sucked on a thick, flavorful hunk of butterscotch. "This is such a bummer. If we weren't afraid of that guy, we could go to The Squinting Cat right now for a game of darts."

Soberly, Jeff nodded. "I'm getting kind of afraid to go outside at all."

The next morning, Aunt Morbelia knocked on their door and said, "Todd? Would you go downstairs in a bit and run up our paper and my tea tray? I am going to wash my hair."

"Sure," he said, glad to have something to do. He'd been staring at the blue-flowered wallpaper for some time, unwilling to read his book. *Dr. Dolittle* was good, but very slow going. Either kids had been much better readers long ago or he was even worse off than he'd thought. He had put the book down and brooded over their problem instead.

Everything that came to mind was wacko or scary or both. As far as he knew, stalkers did not wear hot-pink sweatsuits and have hysterically yappy dogs. They didn't think that a man's golf cap would work as a disguise. Nor did they crack gum, as the young woman had done yesterday afternoon in Salisbury Cathedral. And for sure they didn't wear spike heels that sounded like the pounding of a mad carpenter.

Noisy on purpose, he decided. For the first time he thought of the terrible sounds at Harrowwood in that way. Someone had definitely *wanted* them to hear that moaning in the night. He looked over at Jeff, dying to tell him this newest idea, but Jeff was still motionless under his pillow.

Restless, Todd got up, pulled on his jeans, and ran down to the registration desk in the front hall. Here he was reminded that he and Aunt Morbelia were early risers. The teapots under their flowered tea cosies were still boiling hot, and probably hadn't been there long. Rolled copies of *The London Times* stuck out of the pigeonholes for each room.

But in all of Ye Olde Saxon, only his aunt, Mrs. Dwiddle, and Todd were up. He hadn't ever seen the other guests, a group of German professors now touring the Lake District and planning to return to the B and B for the weekend.

Todd balanced his aunt's tray on his left hand and forearm and grabbed her paper out of its pigeonhole. Two small items tumbled out of the pigeonhole and bounced off the desk, onto the floor. He put down the tray and newspaper and bent over to retrieve what had fallen.

"Birds?" he said out loud, looking at the two feathered toy birds. One was small, with a brilliant red breast and a perky look to its trim, brown body. The other, a bigger bird, had a dull, reddish brown breast and a darker brown body. It was a robin, he knew — Robin Redbreast — although its breast was far less red than the other's. And tied tightly around this one's neck was a hangman's noose.

A miniature hangman's noose made of white string.

He stood, barefooted, and felt his entire body stiffen. The robin had a noose around its neck. No one could mistake the threat. And it had invaded his home in London — his safe place. It was meant to frighten him.

No, he thought. It was in *Aunt Morbelia's* mail slot. They — whoever they were — had sent these beautiful, tiny birds with a very ugly message for his aunt.

Birds, he thought. This pair had dropped out of a pigeonhole. Pigeons at Trafalgar Square. An albatross around Cousin Albert's neck. Girls are called birds here. Ravens at Harrowwood. Ravens in Cousin Albert's journal. More ravens on Tower Green. And now a robin and some other kind of bird.

Angrily, he pounded the desk. He had a lot of patience, more than most, but it was nearly gone. If he didn't find out what was happening — and why — and get it stopped — SOON — he would explode.

He gave the front desk a kick, which hurt his bare foot a lot. Then he stuffed the larger toy bird in his pocket and went to knock on the kitchen door.

Mrs. Dwiddle poked her head out. "Yes, luv?"

"What kind of bird is this?" He held up the small one.

"Ooh, it's a robin, dear. An English robin. Our favorite bird, you know."

Todd's mind whirled, considering the message of the paired birds.

" — how he got his beautiful red breast, don't you?"

"Excuse me?"

"I asked if you knew how he got that bright red breast."

When he shook his head no, she said, "Because he's the bird who plucked a thorn from Jesus' crown of thorns on His way to the cross. And the blood of our Lord stained the breast of the kind little bird, you see." Mrs. Dwiddle's eyes were damp with emotion.

"Even if it isn't true," she went on, "I like to think of our robins that way. Such dear little birds. Ours come sit on our shoulders whenever the major and I whistle."

"I guess ours in America are just bigger."

"And I know why," she said, smiling. "The English folk who settled America were so lonesome for their robins that they called the American thrush a robin — to cheer themselves up, I think."

Todd tried to return her smile. She was a nice lady. But he had to talk to Jeff now. Things were getting out of hand.

"Well, thanks, Mrs. D. I'll take Aunt Morbelia's tea up. See you at breakfast."

He put the English robin in his other pocket and returned to the front hall. He started to pick up the tea tray when the unrolled newspaper caught his eye. Something about the front page was odd, and so he laid it out on the desk to look at it.

Ravens stared back at him. Someone had drawn black, beady-eyed ravens across the top and bottom borders of *The Times*. Ravens with strong, mean-looking beaks.

A few of them had lines floating up to speech balloons, like cartoon characters. One raven said, "Pay attention to those robins."

Another said, "You were warned. Leave before it's too late."

Down in the bottom border, a third raven said simply, "Go home."

First the robins . . . and now this. Open threats instead of subtle games.

Loath to touch it, as if the hate that had gone into its creation would burn his hands, Todd gingerly rolled up the paper and wedged it behind the teapot. He didn't want it coming open where anyone could see it.

Two at a time he climbed the steps to their room. Sounds of splashing water from their shared bathroom told him his aunt was still washing her hair. Hastily he put the tea tray in her room and hurried into his own, where he hid the robins and the newspaper under his pillow.

He ran back downstairs, grabbed a paper from another pigeonhole, ran back upstairs, and put the unspoiled paper on his aunt's tea tray. And now for Jeff.

"Get up," he said, yanking Jeff's pillow away. "We've got big trouble."

Jeff came awake fast as he held the toy birds and listened to Todd. He sat on his bed, legs crossed, and read the ravens' messages while he dangled the American robin by its noose. He gave a whistle as he read, and twirled the little bird around in a circle.

"Quit it!" Todd said, rescuing the thrush-called-robin. It made him tense just to see the thing, let alone have it twirling around dead-like on the end of its noose. What sick person had thought of sending such a warning?

"Bloody birds!" he swore. "Stupid ravens!"

Jeff looked up from the paper. He frowned briefly, then said, *"Ah, what an unfortunate omen. Ravens in the north tower.* Remember when Aunt M said that?"

"Yup. Harrowwood's the answer somehow." Todd thought about going to his aunt right then, but he decided not to. Let her read the paper he had put on her tray and have breakfast. He would get the pictures, and then he and Jeff could present their case with all of the evidence.

Breakfast was almost eerily quiet. Neither Todd nor Jeff could think of anything normal or lighthearted to say. Todd kept seeing the words "Leave before it's too late" in his mind. What had they done to make someone send that threat?

"Todd, are you ill?" Aunt Morbelia asked as the meal dragged on in silence.

"I'm okay." But even as he said it, he sagged back in his chair. No way could he fool her. Once she began probing into something, she always got to the bottom of it.

Now she said, "Something is wrong, Todd, I can tell, and I have all morning to listen. All week, if necessary. Whatever it is, we shall fix it."

He looked at his watch, which said eight forty-five. The pictures were the real clincher, he thought.

Jeff jumped up and pushed his chair back. "You show her what came this morning, okay? I'll get the pictures as soon as the place opens. I've got money and I'll be fine. They don't want me anyway."

Jeff vanished as Aunt Morbelia was trying to make sense of what he had said. "Todd?" she began worriedly.

"It's okay. I'll be right back. I have stuff you have to see." He was gone before she could say anything more.

On his return, he held out the newspaper first. He had hidden the pair of toy robins in his loose sweatshirt and he felt their little wire feet poking his stomach. Just looking at them made him furious. Somebody had a lot to answer for.

Aunt Morbelia's expression grew more severe each second as she quickly surveyed the paper, reading each raven's neatly inked warning. When she looked up, he reached inside his shirt and withdrew the robins. "All this stuff was in the pigeonhole for your room this morning when I went down for the tea. Nobody else was up, except Mrs. Dwiddle, so maybe somebody got in the house. It's all I can think of."

Aunt Morbelia took the birds and examined them, picking at the tiny string noose with one fingernail before setting them down on the paper. "Disgraceful. This sort of behavior is illegal, of course, but it is morally disgraceful as well.

"Todd, what do you and Jeff make of all this? And where in heaven's name has he gone? Is he all right?"

"He's at the photo shop. He'll be back as soon as he gets the pictures I took yesterday."

In slow, careful pieces, Todd advanced his theory. For the first time he told her about the oiled hinges in the gamekeeper's cottage. He explained that he thought they were somehow connected to the horrible noises in the night at Harrowwood, and to the mysterious open windows, and, of course, to all the times that someone had followed them.

Last he talked about the hire car driver, "who's been in on this from the beginning, I think. I couldn't believe it when he was driving the bus yesterday! You'll see when Jeff — " He broke off as he heard the front door slam. "Did you get them?" he yelled.

"Ta da!" Jeff posed in the doorway, one hand out, formally presenting the envelope. "They're terrific, too!"

Todd took out the snapshots and laid them one by one on the table.

Aunt Morbelia tapped the frontal view of the girl at Stonehenge. "Absolutely. This is the girl from the Tower of London." Next she peered at the pictures of the woman.

"Pink warmup suit?" Todd murmured suggestively.

"Oh, saints alive, of course!"

She almost snarled at the picture of the coach driver. "Obviously, I should have heeded the ravens' warning on our arrival, and I shall faithfully listen to you and Jeff from now on. You have known all along that something was amiss, and I have had my head in the clouds. I apologize."

Todd and Jeff grinned at one another and Todd said, "Now what?" He felt as if he had laid down a heavy burden.

"I realize I am responsible for you both, but I

refuse to be intimidated. An interesting idea has occurred to me which I should like to discuss with the Major, but I believe" — one long finger tapped the girl's picture — "I believe we can lay a trap for our little English bird. What do you say?"

"Yes!" they said with one voice.

"What about the others?" Todd asked.

"Somehow I feel sure they will come to her rescue."

12

To Catch a Bird

Aunt Morbelia chose the place. "Hampton Court Palace," she said. "What do you think, Duncan?"

Major Dwiddle brought his eyebrows together in a frown of concentration so profound that Todd expected to hear the gurgle of brain matter. Eventually his eyebrows relaxed and he said, "The maze should be a splendid trap."

Having said that, he went back into a frown. "I assume you have a plan after that. I don't quite see us as torturers, do you, Morbelia? I mean, *gad*, woman, what if she refuses to talk? Then what?"

"You forget, Duncan, that I am a teacher." Aunt Morbelia rose to her feet. She was two inches taller than the Major and considerably more confident.

As she went toward the front desk, she said, "I shall reserve the hire car, wait half an hour, then cancel it, saying that we have decided to go to Hampton Court by British Rail instead. That should guarantee us a nosey parker. This tourist agency must be part of their spy network somehow. I can hardly wait to expose them!"

Todd and Jeff exchanged quick glances. The girl knew where they lived, but they hadn't connected the driver to the tourist agency, which now seemed so obvious an answer.

Following his aunt into the front hall, Todd said, "Do you know who she is? Why do you think she'll follow us today? What if — "

Aunt Morbelia held up her hand, a gesture that silenced him instantly, as it did everyone else who had ever known her. "All in good time, Todd. I shall manage things now, and I hope you and Jeff will stop worrying. We would not be in this fix if I had been a proper guardian. I shall never forgive myself. Thank heavens you two have brilliantly provided us with proof."

"So do you know her?"

Lifting the phone receiver, she said, "No, I do not. I have an idea, but it is unproved as yet. You and Jeff should just relax for a while until I get our trap set. Let me reserve the car now, as I explained."

Todd motioned to Jeff and they went outside, into the back garden. As they checked for hedgehogs around the milk saucers, Todd said, "I don't get it! Why isn't Aunt Morbelia more upset? These weirdos aren't playing games anymore. They're serious, don't you think? I mean, *cckkk!*" He drew an imaginary knife across his throat.

"Yeah, but we've got Major Dwiddle now, so it's four against three. Well, five, if you count Mrs. Dwiddle."

Todd gave him a look.

"Okay, so we won't count Mrs. Dwiddle. What's Aunt M's idea, anyway? What's she going to do with that girl?"

"Make her talk, I guess. Tell us who the others are. Why they're — "

He stopped short at a frantic signal from Jeff. Jeff had wandered off to examine a large garden snail, but now he was forcing his way through some evergreens under a window.

"Come here," he mouthed to Todd.

As soon as Todd neared the shrubbery, he heard his aunt's voice. The open window above the shrubs must be one of several windows at the rear of the parlor, he thought, as he crouched behind the evergreens with Jeff.

". . . clear that I ought to be put in an old folks' home!" Aunt Morbelia was saying. "I have been so preoccupied with the problems of the estate that I did not see — "

"Now just calm yourself, Morbelia," said the Major. "So far, there's no harm done. However, I don't like the tone of this newspaper and these birds. I'd rather call the police — or my friend Beamly, at Scotland Yard. That's it! Why don't we just call Beamly?"

"Not yet, please. After all, I have not completely lost my senses. The girl is their main worker, so to speak, probably because she can keep up with us. We have been moving at a pretty fair clip. So . . . when the tourist agency knows we are going to Hampton Court, I think she will be sent to follow us again. If we apprehend her, we should be able to find out what is going on."

"And if we can't?" he persisted.

"Then we shall have to call in the police."

"*Good,* because this is an altogether shady business! First they tried ordinary intimidation, and now they have stepped up to *outright threats.* I think we're dealing with a *criminal mind* here."

"Perhaps," she replied thoughtfully. "Or maybe just an irrational one."

The voices faded away, and Todd thought they had gone into another room. He and Jeff agreed that Aunt Morbelia knew something she wasn't telling anyone. "Come on," Todd whispered, "I don't want to get caught here."

Back inside, they found Mrs. Dwiddle in her kitchen, whereupon they sat around the table and worried together that Aunt Morbelia's plan might not work. The door to the kitchen opened abruptly as Aunt Morbelia strode in.

"We are ready," she said. "We leave for Hampton Court in fifteen minutes. Duncan knows what to do, Emma."

She stood framed in the doorway, a spare figure, regal and straight, severely dressed in black. Her chin was high and her dark, powerful eyes commanded attention. Todd felt as he had when he'd seen her the first time, on her arrival at his house. This was a truly awesome woman.

Fifteen minutes later, on schedule, Todd, Jeff, and Aunt Morbelia took the Underground to Waterloo Station, where they caught a train to Hampton Court Station. They were obvious about everything, making noisy tourist talk and moving leisurely.

Even so, no one followed them.

As they left the train station and began walking toward Hampton Court Palace, Todd looked back over his shoulder and couldn't believe what he saw. *Nobody.* All the other days someone had been following them and he'd been worried. Now he was worried for the opposite reason.

"Do you believe this?" he grumbled to Jeff.

"Yeah. Where's a stalker when you want one?"

Eyes front, Aunt Morbelia said, "No one, I take it?"
They nodded.

"Then we shall wait around the Lion Gates until someone shows up. It will be perfectly natural to brush up on our facts at the entrance to these historic precincts."

Todd and Jeff put on brave faces and prepared to endure.

"You may be interested to learn that Henry VIII is involved in the story of this palace," Aunt Morbelia began.

"Henry, baby," said Todd. "Every time I learn something about England, Hanky the Eighth was in the middle of it. He sure got around."

She smiled gravely. "Hampton Court was built by Henry's cardinal in the church, a very important man named Wolsey. His palace turned out so splendidly that King Henry *encouraged* Cardinal Wolsey to make him a gift of it."

"Now that's power," Jeff observed.

She started to reply but stopped while a tourist coach disgorged a noisy load of passengers onto the sidewalk.

"Henry VIII always took whatever he wanted," Aunt Morbelia went on, "and he really wanted this palace. Even way back in the 1500s it had a thousand rooms and a staff of five hundred, all waiting on the cardinal hand and foot. What is more, they had indoor water closets. *Jakes* they were called. No one in England had indoor bathrooms as they did here."

Todd perked up at this new information for his research paper on bathrooms. He couldn't believe it — he who struggled with every word in every assignment. To be planning a paper in advance was a miracle.

The babble of the approaching tourist horde brought him back to reality. He had a serious job to do. Maximum serious, he thought, remembering the noose on the toy robin.

He began examining the tourists now milling around them. No, too young. Wrong nationality. Too old. Wrong sex. One by one, he and Jeff rejected the entire group. He lingered over the faces of several middle-aged women, but none was just right.

Stubbornly he began again, face by face. One old, white-haired woman was bent over a cane. In trying to see her face, Todd tipped his head at an angle, and that's when he noticed her hand on the cane. A young hand.

"Check her out," he whispered to Jeff.

"That old lady?"

"Not old. Look at her hands."

Todd moved for a better view of the woman's face, paying special attention to her eyes and nose. And there she was. Behind skillfully applied makeup, in worn, gray clothing and a white wig, there was Miss

Nasty. She was even managing to walk like a stiff, elderly woman.

"There she is," he told his aunt. "Signal the Major and let's head for the maze."

Aunt Morbelia pointed out the little gray lady to the Dwiddles, who were parked at the curb, and then hurried after Todd and Jeff.

Here goes, Todd thought, as they started down the tidy, hedged pathways of the maze. He was surprised at how nervous he was. He kept licking his lips and swallowing. If one of Henry VIII's jakes had been handy, he'd have dashed inside. They just *had* to catch this girl and make her explain.

He and the Major thought alike, he had decided. These people were scary. Who knew what Miss Nasty would do when cornered? What if that cane was a cleverly disguised rifle?

Yes. And then they'd wish policemen were waiting inside the maze, not just a well-meaning, retired Army major.

As they walked between the tall, pruned hedges, Aunt Morbelia said, "The perimeter of the maze resembles a large triangle. Let us see if we can find the farthest point at the back, in the middle of that long leg of the triangle. I believe we should aim for that tree." She pointed with her umbrella.

"Oh dear," she went on, winking at Todd and Jeff.

"I have a pebble in my shoe. Let me lean on you, Todd."

She leaned on him while she pretended to fish for a stone in her shoe. When they saw the gray-clad old lady come around the bend in the hedge, she straightened up. "Ah, that is better. Thank you."

At the first chance to turn, they went right, around a corner, and down a short stretch, then right again, and left. A few more turns and Aunt Morbelia said tensely, "I fear we have ended up in the center, off track."

Todd and Jeff looked at each other. She had told them how easy it was to get lost in this maze. "I know folks who have spent most of an afternoon inside the Hampton Court maze," she'd said. "But I know it quite well, never fear."

Now, her confidence had vanished.

After a few more wrong turns, Todd said, "Come on, you guys. I think I can backtrack."

Up to the end of their path, right for a short ways, then right again, angle left, and ahead of them, down at the end of the path, was a dead end. A cul-de-sac. There, under a tree, and pretending to read *The Times*, stood the Major.

He buried his head further in the newspaper.

Full of his success, though not sure how he had done it, Todd went ahead with the plan. Loudly he said,

"Let's go down there and I'll stand on your shoulders, Jeff, and find the way out."

"Fine by me," Jeff called back.

"Oh, brilliant!" chirped Aunt Morbelia in a forced, unnatural voice.

But when they were all there, in the perfectly placed cul-de-sac, they were alone. They waited for some time, but no old lady with a cane came into view.

Major Dwiddle made a sound of disgust and folded his paper. "Stay here," he hissed, and marched off, whacking his leg impatiently with his paper. They watched him turn left and disappear.

It was fairly dim here and very green. No way out that Todd could see. He slumped with discouragement. It had been a good idea, but somehow it had failed.

"She was in the maze for a while," Aunt Morbelia said, as if reading his mind. "Perhaps she fell behind and lost track of us. Except that we were making enough noise, heaven knows."

Just then, the Major came back into view. He was chatting companionably to the little old lady in gray. One of her hands lay on his forearm and he was patting it, as you would the hand of someone you wanted very much to be with — which was true in this case, Todd realized.

"I had been hoping for a desert campaign," the

Major was telling the old lady. "You know, hunting Rommel the Desert Fox, and all that sort of thing?"

They came closer and closer.

Todd held his breath.

Just a few more feet and she was sure to see them. She would know she'd been led into a trap, as the hedges grew close around them here. Tall, green, impenetrable walls.

Luckily, the woman appeared to be engrossed in what the Major was saying. She hobbled along, looking down at the path, not up. When she did glance up, she and the major were only a few feet away.

Instantly, she straightened. "Crikey!" she squealed.

The Major tightened his grip on her hand and arm. Todd's aunt moved to imprison her other arm.

"Well, now," said Aunt Morbelia, "it is time we had a talk. Come along, and do not make a fuss if you know what is good for you."

The girl's face closed like the door of a shuttered shop, her expression revealing nothing. She paced down the paths of the maze between Aunt Morbelia and the Major as if they were all part of the Lord Mayor's parade. Todd and Jeff followed, shaking with excitement. They had caught their bird after all.

At the Dwiddles' car, the girl unbent only enough to get into the back seat, where she sat erect as an iron poker and just as silent. She managed, with a will that

Todd could only admire, not to look at anyone or any-thing. Rather, she looked beyond them, to some other-worldly place. Remote didn't begin to describe her. She had transcended them.

Todd had seen only one other person behave this way — Aunt Morbelia. When she had first come to live with his family, she had been somewhat like this. Very distant. And sad, of course, because of her sister's recent death. A much *nicer* person altogether, but still . . .

And now his mind was on fire. I knew what to look for today, he thought. Her nose and her eyes. "She has magnificent eyes," Aunt Morbelia had said, that day at the Tower.

Well, of course. He knew who she was.

13

Eyes and Noses, Hands and Hair

In the Dwiddles' car, Todd sat unmoving, staring at Miss Nasty. Jeff was looking at her, too, but Todd could tell he hadn't figured out who she was.

Back at Ye Olde Saxon, the Major and Aunt Morbelia escorted the girl to the desk in the front hall. "Now, young lady," Aunt Morbelia said, "you will telephone your accomplices in this disgraceful business *at once* or we shall call Mr. Beamly of Scotland Yard. Which is it to be? Cooperation or Scotland Yard? Quickly! Time is flitting!"

She was no match for Aunt Morbelia. "Oooh, all right, all right, I'll call them. Our B and B's just round the corner."

Emma Dwiddle shooed everyone else into the dining room. "Get comfy and I'll make us some tea."

"Elevenses, dear!" boomed the Major. "We're hungry!"

When Aunt Morbelia brought the girl into the room, they all sat at a large round table. Todd saw the girl's hands tightly clenched in her lap and watched her eyelashes flutter as she blinked to hold back the tears. He knew that's what she was doing because he'd done it himself.

In the awkward silence he said, "So . . . what's your name?"

She raised her head. "Sibylla. I tell fortunes."

"Oh." He knew he was staring at her, but he couldn't help it. She had contrived to look very old even up close, yet he and Jeff had guessed her real age at about seventeen. When they'd first seen her, Jeff had suggested she was an actress. Jeff must be right, he thought. And now here she was, captured, and staring down at her hands, the one aspect of her appearance that gave her away.

The doorbell rang and the Major leapt to his feet. He came back with the hire car driver — alias the bus driver and the man in the pub — plus the woman in the pink sweatsuit who had worn the flowered dress and golf cap on the Stonehenge tour. And Winston, of course.

"Hrrr, hrrr," growled Winston, who had detected Aunt Morbelia. His strong terrier feet dug into the Brussels carpet as he pulled toward her.

Poised in the kitchen doorway with a loaded tea tray, Mrs. Dwiddle cried, "Oooh, Duncan, my carpet!"

"Bloody dog!" said the Major. "Madam, can't you — "

"Hrrr! Hrrrrr!"

Aunt Morbelia rose up out of her chair. "Silence!" she commanded, pointing at Winston, who sat down and shut his mouth. "Madam, take your dog into the back garden this instant and tie him where he can do no harm."

Nervously the woman nodded and snatched up Winston.

All this time Todd was considering the lean, silent man standing in the entrance to the dining room. One of Aunt Morbelia's old family portraits come to life, he thought.

Knowing the answer beforehand, he nonetheless asked politely, "Albert the Third?"

Face set in darkness, Albert replied, "Indeed." He remained immobile, framed in the doorway.

"*Excellent,* Todd," said Aunt Morbelia. "I am proud to be related to you."

"Thanks." As always, her rare praise was like the conferring of a medal.

"Come in," ordered Aunt Morbelia, nodding at Albert. "Explain why you and your family have followed us. Why you pose as a driver. Everything." She looked from Albert to Sibylla and back again. "I had no idea you existed, you see."

The Major and Mrs. Dwiddle exchanged surprised glances as Albert selected a chair opposite Aunt Morbelia. Albert's deep-set eyes fixed on hers and Todd was struck again by the uncanny resemblance. No wonder Albert's family had used disguises.

Even his hands are the same, Todd realized, looking down at his own long fingers, nearly identical to those of his dad and his great-aunt. The eyes, the noses, and the hands. The hair, too — dark and thick and wavy — and free of a wig now for the first time. Just like Todd's and his dad's, and all pure Fearing.

Tapping the table, Aunt Morbelia said, "I am waiting."

"One wonders about property," Albert said stonily.

She sat up straighter. "If you mean Harrowwood, my sisters and I would have gladly deeded it to you had we known there was a direct heir."

Albert's expression did not change. "My father lived in a big residential hotel with many servants, and I rarely saw him. Then he died. You have what he left me."

Todd and his aunt looked at each other. So Albert did not know that his father's "hotel" had been an insane asylum. And he talks in riddles, Todd thought.

The woman whom Todd still regarded as "the dog

lady," but who he realized now must be Albert's wife and Sibylla's mother, came back inside and sat down next to Albert. "Winston prefers being outdoors. He said to thank you, Morbelia."

"How thoughtful of him," she replied drily.

Albert leaned forward. "When Father lived at Harrowwood, he was immersed in his work, in that tree by the gamekeeper's cottage. It gave him a valuable perspective on the world, he said."

Aunt Morbelia nodded.

"I am there now, continuing his work, as I promised him I would on his deathbed."

Somewhat more gently, Aunt Morbelia replied, "I am glad that someone he loved was with him when he died. Your father and I were very close, long ago."

Todd leaned back, trying to get comfortable, and felt the pressure of the journal between his hip and the chair.

Cousin Albert's journal. Full of the bird sounds that were his "work," no doubt. Now the work of his son. Todd was sure this was the property Albert III wanted most.

He slipped his hand into his back pocket and felt the soft, worn leather of the book he had carried every day since he'd found it. He'd learned to enjoy Cousin Albert's quaint phrasing. The misspellings made him feel comfortable. They had been a link, actually, between him and that odd but appealing ancestor.

But the journal wasn't meant for me, he thought, taking it out of the pocket where it fit so perfectly. He slid it across the table to Albert.

"Here. It was in a dusty old book behind some other books in the library. Probably been there a long time."

With a cry, Albert III grasped the journal and bent protectively over it, his head down.

Moments later, Aunt Morbelia said quietly, "We had no idea."

Albert looked up. "But the ravens' language is in here. You went to speak to them at the Tower. . . ." He blinked, appearing confused, then opened the journal and began to read, as if he were alone in the room.

Todd and Jeff shook hands under the table. Todd had been right and the symbols were important. They were raven talk. *Bird language,* Todd thought. Heck, it could be groundbreaking research, like they say on TV.

In his ear Jeff whispered, "Can you believe this? We were being stalked by your very own family."

Aunt Morbelia waited while Albert read a few pages and then said, "And is it there, the ravens' language?"

He looked up. "Yes. More than I dared hope, and right in our library all these years. Father said something at the last which made me think he'd hidden it in the forest. He had a desperate need to talk with the ravens, of course, to find out what happened to his friend the game-keeper. He suspected that his own father, Albert Leath-erhead, had murdered him, but he died not knowing.

"Now, my job is to tell *all* the birds and animals that human beings are *not like Albert Leatherhead,* not most of them anyway. And I must know the truth of what went before me. I must know!"

"There, there, dear," said his wife.

Albert concentrated only on Todd's aunt. "You see, Cousin, birds have a fairly sophisticated language when compared to deer and hare, which are my next project. Talking with birds is an absorbing challenge.

"But I fear I may never discuss anything of impor-tance with the hare or the deer. They seem, ah" — here he paused — "rather dim-witted. I trust you'll keep that a secret?"

His wife patted his arm. "That was an important point to make, dear. Good for you."

"Egad," said the Major softly.

Again, Todd and his aunt exchanged glances. Al-bert III seemed a lot like his father.

"The drawings?" Todd asked. "Do you know why he drew the birds' heads?"

"Yes, I do. The size and shape of the sinus cavities in a head partly determine the sounds that emerge. Big animals make bigger sounds. Tiny birds make tinier sounds. Father was always very interested in that topic."

"I can tell fortunes now," Sibylla piped up.

"No, thank you," said Aunt Morbelia. "We need answers to questions just now."

"Do call me Betty," said Albert's wife.

"Elizabeth, my queen," said Albert, putting one arm around her shoulder.

"Please!" cried Aunt Morbelia, rattling her spoon against the side of her cup. "Albert, why didn't you just tell me who you were and ask for the journal? Why did first one of you and then another follow us everywhere we went?"

"Oh, it wasn't just us," he replied. "All kinds of different people were following you. So however did you identify *us?*"

"That's the way the British are," added Betty. "No American can stand them for long. You must be about ready to go home by now."

"Rubbish!" barked the Major. "I am exceedingly fond of Americans! Why, in World War II — "

"Thank you, Duncan," said Aunt Morbelia. Turning to Betty she said, "We have pictures of you in your costumes."

Albert shook his head. "And to think we put all of our savings into this desperate plan. . . ."

"Don't apologize, Papa!" Sibylla burst out. "We aren't rich Americans! Harrowwood is all we've got!"

"My dear, a lady never yells," said her father.

"Betty, please," said Aunt Morbelia, "Do explain before we go craz — " She stopped and started over. "Tell us as much as possible, I beg you."

Betty Fearing appeared to gather her forces. "Yes. Well, you see, I work at the estate agent's and so I knew you were coming, and I told Albert I refuse to live in the poorhouse, so we moved out of Harrowwood to the gamekeeper's cottage. You were coming to the house, Mr. Swallow said. But who can pay those rates today? Heavens!

"And so we thought if you saw lots of people being nosey and following you everywhere, you'd hate England and go home and never return and we could move back to our lovely house. And, of course, we were keeping track of Albert's journal. We were supposed to pick it up when you left it on a park bench, or lift it out of your purse, which was silly. I always knew that was a loopy idea."

"Ahhh . . . yes," said Aunt Morbelia, a trifle dazed. She paused, then said, "So you live at Harrowwood secretly because you cannot pay the taxes — the rates. If the authorities knew you were there, you would be evicted for non-payment, correct?"

"I believe so," said Albert vaguely. "Well, no matter. Now that I have Father's journal I shall be the only human who can converse with birds, and our future will be assured. No more dull driving jobs."

Todd was wondering how Albert's talks with birds were going to provide a steady income, when Aunt Morbelia spoke again. "Betty, were you in the loft when we were in the cottage?"

"Yes, thanks to Albert," she said. "He was at work in his tree and saw you coming through the forest."

"That was a hot few minutes, messing the place up, I'll tell you," said Sibylla.

"But we left Harrowwood," said Aunt Morbelia, "and yet you stalked us from then on. Was that because of the journal?"

Albert sat erect. "*Stalking?* I say, that's rude, Cousin Morbelia. We would never stoop to such a thing."

"What do you *think* you were doing?" she retorted.

"Recovering the journal, of course. We also wanted to demonstrate that England would not be a happy place for you to settle — full of rude, nosey people who hate Americans. Betty heard that you live with Todd's family in America. Harrowwood is ours. It is quite simple, really."

"*So is he,*" the Major whispered to Aunt Morbelia. "The wife, too. Logic is a foreign language to them."

Sibylla burst out, "You said you were moving to the cottage — maybe to Harrowwood. Going to fix it all up, you said. It wasn't enough you had the journal, you were going to take our house, too!"

Aunt Morbelia skewered Sibylla with a look. "I merely recommended travel and study abroad to Todd and Jeff. Now, are *you* responsible for the newspaper and the birds?"

Sibylla grew very quiet.

"Oh dear," said Betty. "I absolutely forbade that."

"I know, Mum," said Sibylla. "But I was mad, and when I found the door open, well . . . I just popped in and did it."

For Todd and Aunt Morbelia, words were not necessary. No wonder Winston did as he pleased. So did Sibylla.

Aunt Morbelia took a deep breath. "Well, I must say I am *appalled* by your behavior — all of you. You should have come to me with the truth upon my arrival, and you should have asked for the journal as soon as you knew we had it.

"Stalking is an act of cowards! We Fearings trace our ancestors back to the thirteenth century, and we have been knighted. How could you forget that?"

No one moved. Aunt Morbelia continued grimly. "To atone for what you did, Sibylla, you will scrub every inch of the cottage in the woods, where you and your parents will be living from now on.

"Betty, I suppose the estate could pay you and Albert a small wage if you would act as real caretakers. However, I cannot promise many years in the cottage unless I can find a way to pay the costs of operating the estate. And first, I must hire a new estate agent."

More silence.

"Farley," the Major said abruptly. "Man for the job."

Aunt Morbelia brightened. "As estate manager, you mean? What a good idea, Duncan."

Todd couldn't wait any longer. "Sibylla, did you make those weird sounds in the night?"

"Papa did." She shrugged. "When you went off to follow the sounds, Mum and I popped in to hunt for the journal. We knew you had it, but you came back before we could find it. So we had to leave by the windows. In the *rain*. Such a *pain*." She grinned impishly, all the meanness gone.

Aunt Morbelia set down her teacup. "Albert, did your father teach you to make those frightening sounds?"

Albert nodded. "Yes. Father could make any sound on earth. I have inherited only a small portion of his gifts."

Aunt Morbelia leaned back in her chair, making a steeple out of her long fingers.

"I can hear wheels going around," Todd said.

"Yes. An entire train of thought, actually." She leaned over and whispered. "Todd, they are unusual people, but fascinating. I am sure Albert is a walking encyclopedia on birds and animals, as his father was, and we know they can act parts . . . right?"

"They're great actors, yeah."

She turned to the Dwiddles. "Has Farley considerable management experience?"

"Managed troops for years," said the Major. "Terribly organized chap — knows how to get things done and has a good head for figures. Everyone always likes him, as well."

"Well, then, before we go back home we should have a talk with Farley. Perhaps the estate could become a part-time wildlife school — with tours through the woods and grounds. And lectures by you, Albert?"

Albert leaned toward her, nodding eagerly.

"And sometimes," she continued, seeming to think aloud, "if Farley agreed, you could put on mystery weekends . . . or perhaps mystery lunches to start? Everyone loves a mystery. I quite enjoyed this one — as soon as I realized we had one, that is. And we have the perfect place for all of it — Harrowwood."

"*Yes!*" shrieked Sibylla, leaping to her feet. "Oh, Cousin Morbelia, *yes!* We could put on mysteries, I just know we could! I've always been in plays and I love them, and I would scrub every inch of that place with a toothbrush if we could give it a try! We can make a go of it, I just know — "

"Yes, Sibylla, calm down," said Aunt Morbelia.

"Capital idea," observed the Major. "And Farley's always been terribly keen on nature."

"This's great," Todd said. "Next summer we'll have to come back to see how it's going, right?"

"Yes!" said Jeff, one fist in the air.

"After my talks," volunteered Albert, "I could be the body. The murder victim. It would be restful."

Todd looked closely at Albert. Was that a hint of a smile? Was he teasing? Maybe he had a sense of humor and was a real guy after all, just sort of odd.

"And I will tell fortunes," Sibylla announced.

The doorbell rang and Mrs. Dwiddle left to answer it. As soon as the front door opened, they heard the barking.

Mrs. Dwiddle showed the policeman into the dining room. He had Winston stuffed under one arm. "Neighbor of yours said this dog jumped the fence from your back garden, Major."

"We apologize," said Albert, taking the dog from him. He growled something at Winston, who settled meekly beside him on the floor and went to licking one forepaw.

The policeman beamed around the room. "Americans, I hear. I hope you're enjoying your stay in the U.K."

Aunt Morbelia stood up. "Oh, yes, thank you. A most exciting holiday."

"Smashing!" added Todd.